One Rape, Too Much

"WHY CHILDREN SHOULD NOT RUN ERRANDS FOR NEIGHBORS"

Francis Onyebueze Nmeribe

Dedication

Dedicated to the voiceless victims of rape and child abuse.

Acknowledgments

I acknowledge the help of my daughter, Diana who made time to read through the manuscript when it was still evolving and made useful comments and suggestions that impacted on the book.

About the Author

Francis Nmeribe is a personal transformation teacher, an industrial security expert, and an early retirement planning coach. He holds a degree in Philosophy from the University of Calabar, Nigeria. He is a Fellow of the Institute of Management Consultants (IMC) and a Certified Management Consultant of the International Council of Management Consulting Institutes (ICMCI). He is a Fellow and Certified Security Specialist Instructor (CSSI) of the Nigerian Institute For Industrial Security (NIIS).

He is the author of several career and personal development books including: "Security & Security Guard Handbook", "Principles of Crime Prevention" and "Retire Early To Wealth And Fame."

Other Works of Francis:

- FOUNDATION FOR JOYFUL RELATIONSHIPS
- DATING 101: HOW TO FIND WHO TO MARRY
- GROWING FROM YOUR EXPERIENCES
- RETIRE EARLY TO WEALTH AND FAME
- SEX AND RESPONSIBLITY
- THE ADVENTURES OF BOMBER BILLY
- WHY HOW AND WHEN TO START BUSINESS WHILE YOU STILL WORK FULL TIME

Superscript

The following pages have the despicable experiences of a poor little girl in the hands of men and women who were supposed to protect and raise her who turned around to rape and debase her at every opportunity as told by Mofe Makunjuola, who dared to be different and Sarah herself.

Editors' Note

One Rape, Too Much is a deeply moving and courageous narrative that brings to light one of society's most harrowing and often silenced issues. Through the voice of Sarah, the story does more than recount trauma—it exposes the devastating impact of sexual violence, the struggles of survival, and the resilience of the human spirit.

Francis Onyebueze Nmeribe's storytelling is raw and unflinching, yet it carries an urgency that demands attention. It is a call to action—a plea for awareness, justice, and change. By giving voice to the voiceless and sharing Sarah's journey, this book fosters critical conversations that challenge cultural norms and advocate for those who have suffered in silence.

As editors, we are honored to support the publication of this important work. We believe its message deserves to be heard far and wide, across borders and communities. It is our hope that *One Rape, Too Much* not only educates but also empowers survivors and those willing to stand against injustice.

Chapter One

As told by Mofe Makanjuola

Who is this traumatized but glowing angel?

When I first saw Sarah (I learned her name later that day), her hair was disheveled and dirty, with black and white dust patches all over the exposed parts of her body—her face, arms, and legs below the knees. It was as if she had been sleeping in a barn that had caught fire. She had no shoes on.

My attention was drawn to her when I heard people shouting and mocking her in front of Mama Tosin's table market, where she sells akara, bread, and pap right beside the block of flats where my office is located.

"See small mad woman ooo!" someone shouted.

"Eh! The girl fine ooo. Who go make this one mad now?"

"Get out, mad girl! Who knows wetin you go include yourself inside?" another person yelled.

In a feeble voice, barely audible, she said, "I just want to beg for akara and bread to eat. I am not mad. I have not eaten for many days now—I can't remember how long. I am very hungry," she pleaded.

"Shoo! You even sabi grammar?" another man sneered, hitting her with a stick.

At this point, the physical brutality against this helpless being—who, though disheveled and dirty, still had a glow around her that only I seemed to notice—was too much for me to continue watching from the balcony of my office block.

"Leave her alone!" I shouted from the second-floor balcony and started climbing down.

The man who was about to hit her again stopped, and everyone turned to see who was shouting.

"Ah! It's you, Mofe. Wetin you want with a mad girl?" one of the gathering mobsters asked.

"What has this small woman done to you people that you are mocking and beating her?" I demanded.

"Wo! You no see say she mad?" he asked.

"Even if she is mad, what has she done to you in particular, Badejo, that you are beating her with a stick?"

"Er … Er… she mad now, ah!"

"Please, leave her alone," I said as I reached where they had gathered around her.

She turned her attention to my face, gazed at me steadily, and heaved a sigh of relief. She continued looking at me as though I were her savior.

"Young girl, what is the matter?" I asked.

"Sir, I am hungry. I wanted to beg the madam here for akara and bread to eat. I have not eaten in days, and I don't even know how long that has been," she said.

"Why is a girl like you moving around like this? What is the problem?" I asked.

"It is a long story, and you don't want to hear it," she replied. She now looked helpless, as if the hope of being saved by me was fading.

At that moment, I felt that she was depending on me to help her—maybe just with food, or in some other way.

"You want to eat akara and bread?" I asked.

"Yes," she replied.

"Mama Tosin, give me akara and bread for N100," I requested.

"Ok, Mr. Mofe, but I want cash. You remember say you still owe me N500?" Mama Tosin added.

"Yes, here is N100," I said, handing her the money.

As soon as Mama Tosin extended her hands to give me the akara and bread, the girl looked me directly in the face, grabbed the food between our hands, and started eating while walking away.

"Hey! You have not told me who you are," I called after her loudly enough for her to hear.

"You don't want to know me, sir. All those who did are in trouble—and so am I," she shouted back.

Her shouting and hurried departure made me wonder if she was indeed mad, as people had already claimed.

When she walked a few more steps away from me, I felt a deep sense of personal responsibility to assist her. Her condition and behavior clearly indicated that she needed help.

It was as if something was pulling me to follow her. So, I went after her. I caught up with her and asked her to stop and tell me what had caused a beautiful girl like her, who spoke fluent English, to be roaming the streets barefoot, begging for food.

"Sir, you don't want to know. Please, you are a good man. You saved me from those boys. You gave me food when I was very hungry. I don't even know why I was so hungry that I had to beg for food. I wanted to die so that it would all be over," she said.

"Don't talk like that, beautiful girl. Life is good, you know. It's worth all the trouble to be alive."

"What is there to live for?" she countered. "I don't even know my real age now. I suspect I might be seventeen or eighteen. It has been one terrible suffering after another for as long as I can remember. And you know what? I wish you hadn't come. If those boys and hunger had killed me, it would have been settled. After all, 'Uncle' Tunde, who died, isn't suffering like me now."

At that point, I was confused but also inwardly emboldened to stop her and help her however I could. Before I could finish thinking, I stretched out my right hand, grabbed her by the shoulder, restrained her, and turned her toward me.

"Why is a young girl like you talking about dying? What is the problem? Who is Uncle Tunde? Maybe I can help you if you tell me your story," I said.

"Sir, I have already caused a lot of trouble for people—my father, mother, brother, uncles, aunties, and even others who have met me on the road and tried to help me in their own way." She hesitated, then continued. "You are a good man. I don't want anything to happen to you. Please, go back to your work and let me move on until I die. It seems I am cursed, so dying is the best thing. There is nothing to live for," she stated in a matter-of-fact tone.

"Er … Er… what is your name? If you tell me your story, maybe I could help you," I said again.

She raised her face squarely to mine and asked, "Are you married?"

"No, I am not. Why do you ask?" I responded.

"Because if you are married, I will not come with you. Since you came down from your place and I looked you in the face, I have had this feeling to cling to you for my salvation. But when I remember that all those who took me in during this long travail had problems with their wives—leading to my having to return to the streets where they had picked me up in the first place—I do not want to go into another home, only to be back on the road again shortly, with my suffering worsened."

"Aha! Great. I just wanted to make sure you're okay. I'd like to hear your story."

"I don't think you want to hear my story. However, I'll satisfy your curiosity. I hope that when you hear it, you won't drive me away because it's quite terrible. I also hope that after hearing it, you won't do what other people did, which only caused more problems for both them and me."

"I'll do my best. The only thing I'm curious about is why a beautiful young woman like you would be wandering the streets of Lagos, wishing to die. Let's go to my office. When work is over, we'll go home together so you can take a bath. On the way, we'll stop and buy one or two dresses for you."

"You still haven't told me your name," I prodded.

"My name is Sarah," she responded.

"Sarah who?" I asked.

"My father's name is Enoch."

"Okay, Sarah, come and settle down in the office while we wait for the close of work."

"Thank you, sir," she responded and curtsied.

While she waited, I went down to Mama Tosin and bought her more akara and bread, along with a sachet of water and a Fanta orange. She devoured everything so fast that I began to wonder how many days she had gone without food.

On the way home, we stopped by a small market, where I bought her a gown, a pair of trousers, a T-shirt, and some underwear.

We arrived at my two-room, self-contained apartment late at night after navigating the usual Lagos traffic.

I set up the bathroom for her with hot water, which I had boiled while preparing dinner. We ate in near silence, with me saying only a few words to help her relax. She still seemed on edge and unsettled.

She fell asleep almost immediately on the three-seater sofa in the sitting room. I looked at her and decided to let her be—she needed the rest. She could tell me her story when I returned from work the next day.

While I was getting ready for work the next morning, she woke up and came into the kitchen.

"Is there anything I can do to help?" she asked.

"Go back to sleep, Sarah. It's still too early. I start early to beat Lagos traffic to work."

She quietly walked back to the sofa and lay down again.

I made breakfast and placed it in a warmer. After taking my bath, I went through my usual morning routine—reading the scriptures and praying. I found myself praying for Sarah, hoping she would rediscover herself and regain her sense of purpose.

I woke her up to let her know I was leaving. She looked at me steadily, as if to say, *Are you really going to leave me here alone?*

I assured her that she would be okay.

"Your breakfast is in the warmer. Eat whenever you're ready, and feel free to cook lunch if you want."

"If there's power, you can watch TV or listen to music to keep yourself comfortable. But I recommend that you sleep more so your body can recover. Here's some money in case you need anything that's not in the house," I added.

"When will you be back?" she asked.

"Maybe between 7 and 8 p.m., depending on the traffic."

"Please come back early, okay?"

"Yes, Sarah, I'll try," I said.

"Okay, bye."

As I stepped out onto the street that morning to catch buses and taxis to work, I wondered if she would still be there when I returned.

Throughout the day, I found myself thinking about her. The questions lingered—*What would make a girl like her wander the streets of Lagos in the condition I found her?* I looked forward to finding answers when I got home, hoping she would be rested enough to share her story. My imagination was already building it up as something heartrending. I kept wondering about it for most of the day.

When I returned, I was stunned. Sarah looked like a completely different person—more mature and even more beautiful. She had taken excellent care of the house.

She had tidied up the rooms, including my bedroom, changing the bedspread and pillowcases that hadn't been replaced in weeks. She had swept, mopped, and even freshened the air with deodorizer.

It *felt* like a home.

She had also taken care of herself. She was dressed in the jeans and T-shirt I had bought for her the previous evening, and she had even applied light makeup, enhancing her already beautiful features.

"Wow! Did a genie visit while I was at work?" I asked, astonished.

"Yes, a genie came and told me to sleep. When I woke up, everything had been fixed—including me and the food."

"Hmmm," was all I could say.

"I bought some makeup with the money you gave me. I hope you're not mad?"

"No, not at all. In fact, I love how you look with it."

"What would you prefer to do first—take a bath or eat? Both are ready. Do you prefer hot or cold water? I prepared both," she said, smiling shyly.

"Wow, Sarah, it's like you read my mind! When it rains like it did today, all I want is hot water for a bath. But usually, by the time I start thinking about how to prepare it, I just give up and go without bathing. Thank you."

"It's nothing. I just want to be useful again. It's been so long since I've done something meaningful… ever since I ended up on the streets."

"Stop right there, Sarah. No more grieving from now on, okay?" I said firmly.

"Okay, thank you, sir. Go and take your bath now. After dinner, I can tell you my story—if you're still interested. But be warned, it's a long one. It might take a few days to finish, and you may not like me after hearing it."

"No problem. I'd be glad to hear it. See you shortly," I responded.

After immersing myself in a sweet, warm bath, I felt very refreshed and truly happy.

We ate one of the best meals of jollof rice and fried plantain I had ever had since leaving home for Lagos in search of a job. She had added stockfish head to the rice, making it taste just like my mother's cooking. I ate more than my usual fill.

When she took the dishes to wash, I felt an intuitive nudge to join her. We washed the dishes together, stealing glances at each other from time to time.

When we were done with the dishes, we sat down opposite each other on the sofas in the sitting room. I noticed she seemed a bit fidgety. It was clear she was struggling with the burden of telling me her story.

"Well, Sarah, would you mind soothing my curiosity by telling me your story?" I asked.

"Yeah… That's what's been on my mind—what I should tell you and what I shouldn't. I fear that when you hear my story, you'll throw me out of your house like garbage," she said.

"I promise you, I would never do anything like that. In fact, let me assure you that my desire to hear your story is no longer just about curiosity. I truly want to know who you are," I said.

"I will tell you everything. But where do I begin? It's long and painful," she said.

"Start by telling me about your childhood—anything you can remember. Tell me about your father, your mother, and your siblings, and then how your journey led you to where we met," I said.

Chapter Two

As told by Sarah

Me, as I remember before that fateful day.

I remember that I just enjoyed life—or let me say, being alive—because back then, I didn't really know the difference. I was happy with my mother. I was happy with my father. I was happy with my brother, James, especially since he is much younger than me, and I didn't have to compete with him like other girls my age do with their own siblings who are almost the same age as them.

Special times in my life included when my mom returned from the market and brought me some secondhand clothing that looked pretty on me. I always felt good each time I wore one of these new dresses. My mother was always bringing me dresses, underwear, and earrings, and they always made me happy to have them.

I looked forward to Sundays because we ate a special meal of rice with cow meat instead of the iced fish that often graced our soup and stew.

I was happy to go to the nearby private school, where our class was so small that everybody knew everybody, including our parents. I came in first place one or two terms each year. The aunties and uncles who taught us thought I was brilliant. I was happy to be brilliant. I felt on top of the world each time I came first in my class—or on the one occasion when I came first overall in the whole school while in primary four.

Shortly before the fateful day, I had just blushed for the first time when one aunty in our compound told another, "This Mr. Enoch's daughter is pretty." I had a lighter complexion than my not-so-light-skinned parents, who wouldn't be considered dark-skinned either.

I was on the bigger side for my age. I had my father's lanky frame and my mother's beautiful looks. My body parts and female features, like my breasts, seemed bigger than those of my age mates.

Growing up, I thought my mother worked too much and my father too little. My mother always seemed to have money to buy the little things we needed. At first, I thought my father brought nothing home and eventually had to ask my mother one day. That was when she sternly warned me never to belittle my father in my thoughts or words because he was a good and great man. She explained that they both ran the same shop in the market and that he allowed her to hold and manage the money. That day, my young mind wondered about fathers and mothers. I revered my father in an intrinsic way—in a way I couldn't quite comprehend or express.

Today, with my current age and experience, I think I admired and adored my father very much.

I counted myself fortunate to be born to goodly parents. It was worth much more than any earthly possession my small mind and heart could comprehend. I felt good about myself.

Now, looking back, I can describe myself as vivacious, gorgeous, happy, and pretty—okay with living in two rooms with my parents in a large compound where we shared bathrooms, toilets, and a kitchen with other families.

Chapter Three

My father, as I remember him before that fateful day.

He was a tall, slim-built man—not so light but not so dark-complexioned. I could never really imagine his age. He always looked young in my eyes, especially since he smiled and laughed more than he shouted or quarreled. He talked very little. The loudest you would hear his voice was when he was laughing or singing songs from his native land, which he proudly recounted as the songs they grew up with in their youthful days.

I was always in awe of what his youthful days could have been like if he was so graceful now. As my mind and physical eyes gained more understanding, I noticed that my father had some strands of gray hair, which my mom always accused him of getting from suffering rather than aging. When his face was not covered by his usual happy expression, you could see traces of strain that must have resulted from hardship and struggles in his younger days.

My dominant image of him was that of a gentle, cool, and somewhat lazy person. My judgment of him as lazy came more from my mother's rather wild and fierce behavior than from his actual actions. I had expected him to be the wild one and my mother the gentle one.

Other fathers in our neighborhood were fierce, often mistreating their wives and beating their children. My father, on the other hand, was extremely fond of my mother and hardly ever raised his hand against me. The idea that he was lazy faded the day my mother informed me that my father was an equal partner in their trading business—one I had originally thought she owned alone.

To my father, I was a jewel. He treasured me. He spoke about me proudly all the time, and I felt welcome in his company, often sitting on his lap and playing with his mustache. He called me by many pet names—"Gold, Treasure, Pearl, Angel, Jewel," and more. My mother always teased him, wondering how he never ran out of new names to call me. Each time he called me these names, my heart melted. I now recognize that as affection, but back then, I didn't fully understand what those feelings meant.

One time, my mother asked me to wash the dishes. I looked at the dirty plates, covered in oil, vegetables, bones, and remnants of last night's soup. I imagined putting my hands into cold water on that chilly morning, and I refused. When my mother started shouting and beating me, I still wouldn't budge—I just kept crying.

Then came my father.

He spoke in his usual playful way: "Who is making my angel upset this morning? Do they not know this is the father's own treasure? Come on, my sweet daughter! What is the matter?"

I seized the moment and ran to him. He bent down, hugged me, and I fell into his arms, resting my head on his shoulder. I felt peace.

Stroking my hair, he gently asked, "What do you want to do about the errand your mother gave you?"

Because of his approach, I found that I could no longer say I wouldn't do it. Instead, I simply said, "The water is cold."

"Can I boil some water for you to use in washing the plates?" he asked. "The hot water will help dissolve the oil and make the plates easier to wash."

"Yes, Dad," I quickly responded.

He settled me on a chair in the backyard and brought me slippers so I wouldn't have to walk barefoot on the cold, wet ground. Then he went into the kitchen and placed water on the stove to boil. My admiration for him grew.

All the while, my mother kept eyeing me as she walked past. Each time she returned to the backyard, she would throw in a comment or two to taunt me.

Though I cannot classify my father as rich or highly educated, he was the greatest father any girl could ever have.

Chapter Four

My Mother, as I remember her before the fateful day

My mother was not a tall woman compared to my father. However, she was larger than life in my mind. Where my father was quiet, my mother made sure she was heard loud and clear. One of the things I adored about her was her figure—she had a body that made her look younger than her age. My father often said that I took after her in beauty.

In those days, I didn't fully understand what beauty meant. But I was always proud of how my mother looked, especially compared to the other mothers in the large compound where we lived with many other people. She always took care of herself, paid attention to her appearance, and smelled good all the time. I loved hugging her—when she wasn't sending me on errands or scolding me for not doing what I was told, for doing something badly, or for doing something I wasn't supposed to.

She walked tall and confident and talked fast. There were no dull moments with my mother.

I remember when she was pregnant with my younger brother, James. Her stomach bulged, but I didn't really understand what was happening. Despite her pregnancy, she still carried a big four-gallon water container to fetch water from the nearby public borehole. If anyone dared to stand in front of her or tried to stop her when she believed it was her turn, she would tongue-lash them, push them aside, fetch her water, and even fill my one-gallon container for me. It didn't matter whether they were men or women—everyone got the same treatment.

One day, after she pushed a man aside to fetch her water, he said, "Woman, carry that belly and go meet the man who did this to you… don't come and involve me in it, o."

My mother fired back, "If you call yourself a man, come and touch me and see fire right now."

On our way home, I asked, "Mommy, which man did your belly like that? The man was laughing at you."

"Hush!" she snapped. "Don't put your mouth in that kind of thing."

The vehemence in her voice was so frightening that I dared not ask again.

However, I got my chance to ask my father. He stopped, thought for a moment, and then said, "Well, I don't think you should know about this kind of thing yet. But your mother is pregnant with a child.

She will have another baby—he will be your brother if it's a boy, or your sister if it's a girl."

"Which man put it inside her belly?" I asked.

After a long silence, my father said, "I put it inside your mother."

"Oh! Did you put me inside Mommy like that before I came out?"

"Yes, my gold. Everybody was born that way, except Adam and Eve."

Whatever my father told me always comforted me, whether I understood it or not. Just like this time, I wasn't sure I understood his explanation, but I was happy that I would have a brother or sister. Many other girls in the compound had little siblings they dragged around.

The next time I was alone with my mother, I said, "Mommy, it is Daddy that did your belly like—"

Before I could finish, she had already landed a slap on my face.

"What have you been asking your father, you witch girl?!"

"Do not ever talk about those kinds of things again," she commanded.

"Yes, Mommy," I sobbed.

My mother naturally exhibited power, and that made her even more admirable to me. Though I wished she dealt with me less harshly, I secretly wanted to be just like her. Especially since, in my early years, I had thought my father was lazy because of his quiet disposition. My mother was the exact opposite. In hindsight, my father's calm nature was probably the reason they lived together so peacefully.

My mother always won arguments. I remember some typical scenarios: When my father made a statement and my mother countered it, he would smile and restate that he meant what he said. My mother would always cut in and insist she didn't believe him. I cannot recall my father ever restating anything for the third time. The matter always ended when my mother insisted she was right. On those occasions, I could tell that my father knew he was right but didn't want to fight—he would simply smile and say nothing more.

Despite their arguments, I knew my mother loved and respected my father. She never joked about his welfare. Many times, after meals, she would lean on him and rub the hair on his legs. I also caught them kissing several times, and though I couldn't put my feelings into words back then, those moments made me feel… something.

A good name for my mother would be "workaholic." Even though she was in the market with my father daily, she always returned earlier to do the household chores. She never let my father do any domestic work, even when he wanted to help.

She would always say, "Oh, Enoch, my good husband, let me do this one for you, oh!"

Chapter Five

My Younger Brother, James

When my brother James was born, it was one of the most hectic times in our house. For the first time, my father called me to help with some chores. For the first few days, my workaholic, strong mother appeared weak.

She sat or lay on the bed most of the time, always carrying the baby and giving him her breast to suck. I chuckled each time I saw them like that, feeling a mix of emotions. It surprised me to see my mother so calm, giving personal attention to the little boy.

I couldn't remember being in that state myself. Sometimes, when I watched the two of them, I wondered if she had done the same for me. One day, I summoned the courage to ask her. I must tell you, asking my mother a question was never easy for me. But I was so moved that I couldn't help but ask. For the first time in my life that I could remember, my mother responded with tenderness.

"Mommy, did you do what you're doing for this child for me when I was small like him?"

"Sarah, baby girl, come!"

With some trepidation, I stepped closer. She drew me in and held me warmly. I felt a glow inside me.

"When you were born," she said, "you were so cute and small like your little brother. I was happy to have you, and I did exactly the same thing for you. It is called breastfeeding. Your father is the most wonderful man on earth. He cared for me so much, and I was happy to care for you just as much."

"Wow!" I could hardly believe it or fully comprehend it. However, something inside me shifted that day. I realized that my mother cherished me, despite everything I had felt about her 'harsh' ways with me.

So, James became the source of a revelation for me. This caused me to develop a special affection for him.

As soon as he was able to play with me, he was mine all the time. In our little, childish ways, we bonded very well. When we were together, James rarely looked for Mom or Dad. It seemed I was enough for him—unless he was hungry, needed water, or had wet his pants. When he grew old enough for me to feed him, I became even more essential to his daily life, at least when he wasn't sick or teething.

For me, James meant joy.

That's why, very early in his life, my parents trusted me enough to leave both of us at home on weekends when I wasn't in school.

Chapter Six

Uncle Tunde as I saw him before the fateful day.

"Uncle" Tunde was a tall man—neither handsome nor ugly—who came to live in a one-room apartment in the large compound where we lived. I did not know where he came from or even which tribe he belonged to. We were not related in any way. The title 'Uncle' was simply the common way we addressed older people, whether or not they were actually our parents' siblings.

He was a friendly man who always touched people while greeting them. He liked having the young girls in the compound hug him, and he was always carrying children and hugging them as he came and went.

By the time he arrived in our compound, I had reached an age of self-consciousness. I never let him hug me. I don't remember my exact age then, but my breasts were starting to develop, and pubic hair was growing around my vagina. Many times, he tried, and each time I escaped from him, he would stand there for a while, looking me over before moving on to play with the other children or leaving the scene. I often wondered what he felt or thought each time that happened.

But he was good—or should I say 'nice'—with children and played with us often. Some evenings, he would sit in front of his door, facing the open space in the yard, and many children would gather around him as he told us all sorts of stories. We felt happy in his presence. Today, I understand that to mean we liked him in our innocent, childlike way. He was fun to be with.

He often called the little boys and girls in the compound to run errands for him. Some even fetched water for him. Sometimes, he walked with us to fetch water, always making sure we filled our containers before he got his own. He even helped us balance our water on our heads before picking up his own two small gallons, which he carried in his hands.

He taught at a nearby public secondary school and often helped the children in the compound with their homework. He was always involved with the kids in one activity or another. At least, that was all I knew of him from my not-so-close but generally good relationship with him.

The only times when 'Uncle' Tunde wasn't surrounded by children were at night when he was sleeping and one weekend every month when a big lady visited him. Each time she came, usually on Friday evenings, we would hardly see 'Uncle' Tunde until Sunday evening, when he escorted her out of the compound.

In my judgment then, "Uncle" Tunde, as we all called him, was a good man.

Chapter Seven

One rape, too much, the day that turned life upside down.

The first time I ran an errand for Uncle Tunde, he sent me to buy pap and akara for him. When I returned and knocked on his door, he emerged from his room as if he were going out and asked me to place the pap and akara on the center table. By the time I turned, he was right behind me. He held me and started touching my body—my small breasts and buttocks. It felt sensitive and confusing at the same time, and that made me afraid.

I told "Uncle" Tunde that what he did was scary and that it didn't feel good, but he assured me that he knew how to make it "sweet" if I would just relax. I refused to relax and ran away. As I escaped from his room that day, I had a strong feeling that what he tried to do to me was wrong.

My mother is a great woman. I adored her very much. But she was not someone I could discuss anything concerning my body or sexual organs with. She hushed me at any mention of such things in a way that made it clear they were off-limits—or at least, that's how I felt.

When I first felt sensations as my breasts started growing and mentioned it to her, she didn't let me finish describing my feelings. She shut me up and gave me a look so frightening that I understood it to mean, Do not dare. So, I never dared to bring up what "Uncle" Tunde did to me—how he touched my breasts and buttocks and how it felt—not with her or with anyone else.

If only I had tried to bring it up, maybe the calamity that followed would not have happened.

There was nothing about that fateful day to suggest that it would be the last day of my peace and happiness—the beginning of many years of trauma, wandering in the wilderness of life, with my father in prison, my mother insane, and my brother James separated from me.

Before this incident, we had a life I now know was very sweet. It was simple. There was no wealth of any kind. In fact, we were clearly poor and needy, but nobody knew because my mother and father cared deeply for each other, for James, and for me. They always made up for one another. I never heard or saw my mother demand anything from my father. They would sometimes talk seriously about their business or how to manage food for the week, but they never argued over money or anything else. It was different from the other women in our compound, who often quarreled and fought with their husbands over food money and all sorts of domestic issues. Sometimes, the fights ended with the women getting beaten.

Our life was simple and sweet. That is how I would describe it now, knowing what I know.

Even if there had been signs that trouble of such magnitude was coming, I probably wouldn't have understood them at my age. I was almost eleven years old when this happened. Now, I am seventeen, going on eighteen.

My mother and father had gone to the market that Saturday morning. Since James had grown a little, my mother felt comfortable leaving him at home with me on Saturdays. I loved taking care of James, so I was happy to have the day with him. I was eight years older than James.

When "Uncle" Tunde called me to buy him akara and pap that morning after my parents had left, my mind went back to the last time—his attempt to touch my body. A part of me told me not to go on that errand. Without a clear picture of the danger I faced, I battled with my thoughts before deciding to go.

James had fallen asleep a little while before "Uncle" Tunde called me. I laid him on the bed, covered him with wrappers, and left to answer the call.

When I got there, he handed me some money to buy akara and pap from Mama Bisi, who sold in front of our compound. I bought the food and returned. When I knocked on his door, he invited me in, saying he was holding some tools and that I should place the items on the center table.

As soon as I stepped inside and headed for the table, he quickly crossed to the door and locked it. Then he turned around and started calling me names—"Sweet girl, beautiful girl, look at your eyes." His words made me blush. I was about eleven years old and had started developing breasts and pubic hair, which made me more aware of my body. His flattery affected me. Maybe it even lessened my fear about why he had locked the door.

When it came to what men could do to a woman's body, either willingly or by force, I was completely innocent. I couldn't really imagine it.

"Uncle" Tunde, why did you lock your door? I need to go out. My little brother James is all alone, I said.

"Come, sweet girl. Don't worry about your brother."

When I handed him his change, he told me to keep it.

"No, 'Uncle' Tunde, I cannot keep the change," I said.

"Why not?" he asked.

"I even bought you some gifts. Here, take!" He handed me a plastic digital watch, a pack of sweets, and some biscuits.

"I'm sorry, 'Uncle' Tunde, but I can't accept your gifts. Who will I tell my parents gave them to me?"

"You don't need to tell your parents. Hide them and enjoy them."

"No, I can't," I said and turned to leave.

He grabbed me tightly with one arm, and I screamed.

"Uncle" Tunde, you're hurting me! Leave me alone!"

All the while, his right hand had been clenched in a fist as if he planned to hit me. He held me tighter. As the alarm of danger—though I had no idea what was coming—rose within me, I started crying. He placed his right palm over my mouth and nose, as if to say, *don't cry*, and to wipe away my tears.

I perceived a sharp smell. I must have passed out instantly because I knew nothing after that, and for how long, I cannot remember.

The next thing I remembered was hearing my little brother, James, screaming from across where our apartment was.

As if from a dreamland, I started returning to consciousness and saw myself lying alone, unable to move a limb, and in the sourest pain I had ever felt in my vagina and thigh. When I cried out, *Uncle* Tunde appeared from outside the door, locked it, and helped me sit up. He must have taken time to clean up the mess he had made of my vagina while I was still passed out. I could smell antiseptic and saw pieces of cloth and tissue paper on the ground, stained with blood.

I heard myself say, "You call yourself my uncle? Look at what you have done to me. How do I face my mother?" I cried.

Uncle Tunde said, "Oh no, don't tell your mother. If you tell her, there will be big trouble. Both of us may die."

As soon as I could gather myself, I struggled—with *Uncle* Tunde's help—to move to our apartment and managed as best as I could to attend to my little brother. I could not help him much because I needed help myself just to move, but there was no one I could call. And even if there was, I didn't have the confidence to ask for help. What would I even say was happening to me? I prayed that the pain would go away before my mother returned and that I might be able to walk normally so no one would notice.

The soreness around my vagina felt as if someone had used a knife to cut it. Any movement of my hands and legs ached like hell.

But despite all the pain, this was merely the beginning of my nightmare.

My mother returned first, as was always the routine. I could not run out to welcome her as usual, and that got her worried.

She screamed, "Sarah! What is wrong with you? I came back, and you won't come out to receive me? Are you all right? Or have you gone mad?"

Her questions shot at me like spikes as she approached. I did not get up from where I was. I just cuddled my little brother as if it was him that kept me from coming out. But as soon as he heard and saw our mother, he jumped down from my lap and ran to her. His movement caused me agonizing pain, and I muffled a scream.

The truth came out when, even after James ran to my mom, I did not get up. My mother could no longer hold herself. Both out of fear that I had fallen ill and in anger that I could just sit there when she returned, she shook me and demanded to know what was wrong.

All I could do was burst into tears.

She watched in bewilderment as I continued to sob, tears pouring down my cheeks. After a moment that felt like an eternity, she dropped my younger brother and picked me up. The pain was so unbearable that I screamed louder.

I noticed her sniff me, and the next moment, she pulled up my gown.

I had no underwear on. *Uncle* Tunde must have used it to clean me up, or he had kept it. And the evidence of the damage he had done to my vagina was there for her to see.

She screamed, "Eewooooooooooooooooooo!" so loud that I became more afraid than I had been before. I can still hear that scream to this day, and her cry has continued to haunt me.

"Who did this to you?" she demanded.

I kept crying.

"Who did this to you?" she asked again, louder this time.

I still cried, unable to speak.

Uncle Tunde had said that if I mentioned it to anyone, both of us would die. So I kept crying instead.

Then she said, "Before you kill me, I will kill you with my own hands."

She slapped me hard across the face, making me fall sideways, then charged after me for more.

I screamed, "I am dead, ooo! Mommy, I will tell you!"

"Yes, go ahead and tell me!" she shouted.

"It's *Uncle* Tunde."

"Did he come here to do this to you, or did you go to his room?"

Through my sobs, I answered, "I went to his room, ooo! He sent me to buy him akara and pap, and he started touching me."

Through heavy breaths, she beat me more.

"You have killed me, Sarah, so I have to kill you!"

"You have disgraced me, Sarah, so I have to kill you!"

"You have brought shame upon me, Sarah, so I have to kill you with my own hands!"

All the while, she kept beating me. My little brother was now crying uncontrollably.

Many neighbors gathered in and outside our sitting room.

It was in this chaos that my father came in. He stopped my mother from the temporary insanity that had seized her. When he was finally able to pull her away, she started crying uncontrollably as well.

The whole small room was now saturated with wailing. Neighbors had started returning to the compound, and they poured into our room to ask what was wrong.

The shame and public ridicule were unbearable. My father, upon hearing my mother's explanation through her sobs, bowed his head, and I saw tears falling from his eyes to the ground.

Then, more neighbors poured in. At times, they all asked their questions simultaneously. Some of those close to our family received explanations from my mother amid her increasing wailing and gnashing of teeth. However, when those who were not particularly kind to us inquired, my mother would not respond but instead wailed louder. Bystanders would then begin explaining to them.

Some rumors spread that I had gone to 'Uncle' Tunde and that he had raped me. Others would say things like:

"Nobe that gal wey im eye dey sharp like oku elu, Sarah? Wetin e do?" someone or many would ask at once.

"E don carry herself go give that foolish schoolteacher, Tunde, wey no know his mate. E don carry his thing wey no dey rest go spoil the small girl.

Children wey no dey hear something!

E be like say they send am to come kill her innocent mother."

Another neighbor interjected, "Oh my God! If to say I shout for the whole compound the other day, ooo, maybe I for save my neighbor and im daughter from this useless man, Tunde. Ahhh! That useless man, Tunde! I no know who make am teacher, ooo! No be two weeks ago wey my daughter wey never grow hair for vagina come report to me say that 'Uncle' Tunde call am say make im come help am buy akara and pap for Mama Bisi place. As she bought the akara and pap come give am, naim that useless man come begin touch her for breasts and bombom, come dey tell am say she fine well well.

One time, one time, I shout my daughter down. I say, that man no be your uncle anything, joor. He come from Ijesha, we we come from Abeokuta. We no relate, sam sam. E no be my brother. E no be your papa brother. So, e no be any uncle, jareh! Naim that day, I come call my children tell them make they no do any message for anybody for this compound again. I tell them say, this na township. As we live for one compound, no be say we be relation!"

As more and more people poured in, my mother increased her crying. I was dumbfounded, confused, ashamed, and unable to comprehend anything more.

Some of those who came mocked, "See am for you! See am for you, Mama Sarah. Person wey no dey stay house look your child, see am for you."

Others accused, "As mama goat dey chop and chew, na im the pikin go dey watch am na."

At this point, my father lost it.

He wailed, "Aaaaahhhhhhh!!!!"

To this day, I can still hear my father's cry, the one he let out as he sprang to his feet, grabbed a machete from under the bed, and dashed outside.

Tunde may have been standing near his door, listening to all the commotion in our house. Before the neighbors could react and chase after my father, I heard a loud bang at the door, a wail, and then a thud on the ground, followed by groans and my father's shout:

"E woo! I have killed somebody, ooo! Ahh! This world!"

My father continued repeating, "E woo! Ahh! This world!" for as long as I remained conscious.

Some men overpowered him and took the machete from his hands. They sat him down. Some reprimanded him, while others sympathized.

"Enoch! Nobe so," one man said. "What the man did na small thing. This one wey you don do now, na im be worse."

"Heyi! Enoch, you don enter mud. Before government people finish with you, e go better for you to watch see the man do that thing to your wife and daughter at the same time," another man said.

The way everything unfolded, no one spoke about my sexual abuse, my age, or my rape by 'Uncle' Tunde. The only thing that filled the air was that my father had killed Tunde.

The whole compound was packed with people. Confusion was everywhere. My mother, I, and other close friends were dumbfounded. We just stared blankly ahead. For me, I was sure my eyes were open, yet I saw nothing—not even the crowd. There was just a haze over my vision and an overwhelming noise around me.

One good neighbor took my younger brother, James. In all the chaos, I doubted we even remembered he existed.

Then, the police arrived and took my father away in handcuffs. That roused me. I cried and ran after them until they pushed me back and forced him into their vehicle.

I kept shouting at them, "That is not what happened! That is not what happened!"

I am sure they did not make sense of what I was saying. They ignored me and went ahead. I wanted them to hear the whole story, but they would not listen.

Nobody wanted to listen.

It has been about seven years now, and nobody—except you— has agreed to hear me out.

Nothing in my life prepared me for the trauma and misfortune that this one single rape by "Uncle" Tunde has caused my family and me.

The police came back later to remove Tunde's body from the compound.

I do not know how we survived to the next day. Then the police came back for me. When they took me, my mother insisted on coming. She also brought food for my father.

When they brought my father out of the cell, he had chains on his legs and hands.

I could not comprehend it. My father was not a violent man. In fact, as I was growing up, I thought he was too quiet for a father. While the other fathers in the compound quarreled and fought with their wives and children—shouting and beating them—my father hardly ever argued with my mother. I had thought the violence these men inflicted on their wives and children was what made them manly.

The sight of my father being led out of the cell in leg and hand shackles made my mother and me start crying instantaneously. He told us to stop crying, saying we had a lot of time ahead and a lot of trouble.

My mother gave him food. She asked whether there was any word that Tunde had survived.

"I don't know," my father replied helplessly.

"Don't worry, I will ask the police before we leave here today," my mother assured him.

Not fully appreciating how much Tunde's survival related to my father's freedom, I wished him dead, and I said so.

"I wish he dies for bringing all of this upon us."

"Hush!" my mother scolded.

"Do you not know that if he dies, your father would be killed for killing him?" she asked in a matter-of-fact tone.

"Ahhhhh!" was all I could say in bewilderment.

Uncle Tunde did not survive the machete cut he got from my father. They said his head was almost torn in two, making survival impossible.

I cannot recount the grueling experience my mother, my brother, and I endured while my father's trial lasted.

In the end, he was convicted of killing "Uncle" Tunde and sentenced to seven years of imprisonment with hard labor, without any option of a fine. They said he was convicted of manslaughter. If it had been murder, he would have been hanged until he was dead. The judges believed he had been provoked into his fatal actions.

That day in court, they allowed him to hug us before taking him away. He told me he was sorry and asked for my forgiveness. I wondered at him. I was the mess here. I was the one who should be apologizing. That confused me even more, and my mouth just hung open as tears flowed involuntarily and profusely.

He called my mother by a name I had never heard before.

"Crown of my head, please be strong, I pray you. Take care of these two little angels God sent to us."

My mother did not say a word. She just continued to cry until the police officers and prison warders took him away from our grip. Even James, who was just a small boy, was wailing uncontrollably.

The next month was torture for all of us. My mother, James, and I were inconsolable. My grandmother—the only one I knew to be my mother's mother—came and took us away to her home in the village. She lived alone, having lost her husband a few years earlier.

Life with her was difficult. She blamed me for everything, constantly reminding me that I had been the ruin of the family from the time I was conceived to this final destruction.

She recounted how I was the reason my father had married my mother in the first place.

She told the story: "When your mother was young, she said she loved this man. We warned her that the man was poor and that she should wait for Alpheus, the son of the cocoa merchant in the village, who loved her but had traveled to the big city to go to a big school. Your mother would not listen. The next thing we knew, she announced she was pregnant for this poor man and was moving in with him. When your father came to marry her, I did not accept his gifts. They married anyway, and some months later, you were born. So, you are trouble. I saw it coming, but nobody would listen to me. Now, you evil child, you have destroyed your own father."

Every day, for most of our stay with Grandma, I made efforts to avoid her.

My mother could not handle the trauma. She kept blaming herself. One day, she told me how she believed it was her fault.

"Maybe if I had covered you and secretly cared for you—maybe, just maybe—we would have forgotten that you were raped. Maybe your father wouldn't have known. And maybe he wouldn't have murdered Tunde. Look at how my impatience with others and my headlong approach to things have ruined my family—my sweet family. We had nothing, but we were happy. We had nothing, but we were at peace. Sarah, my sweet husband's angel, I am sorry," she lamented.

Then she started blaming herself every day.

Before long, she was unable to coordinate herself. She lost it. She would suddenly spring to her feet and shout my father's name—

"Enoch! Enoch!! Enooooch!!! Ahhhhh!"

Then she would start crying. This continued for several days and weeks, and nobody could console her.

One day, she went berserk. She threw off all her clothes and ran out almost naked. Many villagers gathered. They brought her back, but my grandmother, worn down by age, was unable to bear what was happening. It was decided that some people should take James and me to care for us.

By this time, it had been about a year since Tunde drugged me, tore my vagina apart, and shattered our world—leading to my father being jailed and my mother losing her mind.

Chapter Eight

The Days of Wondering in the Wild

One day, some weeks after my mother was taken away to a native doctor's home, a woman was introduced to me as my aunt—a true aunt this time, as she was my mother's older sister. She took James and me to her home in the big city.

Living with Aunt Sarah in her big city home was a transformation for us. I looked forward to an opportunity to return to school and hoped that my brother James would be able to go to school. The heat and confusion of the past year had made it impossible for him to start school and for me to return. I had already missed one school year. I was full of hope that I would be able to have a life again.

Aunt Sarah and my mother were my grandmother's only children.

Aunt Sarah—I later learned that I was named after her—was the only person who supported my father's marriage to my mother. It was as if my grandmother wanted her to come and carry the trouble she had helped bring about years ago.

She was married with two grown children, both boys. I said they were grown in the sense that they were bigger and older than me. Both were in university at the time. Her husband was much older than my aunt, but they seemed to do well together. They were happy most of the time. The man was quite educated. He seemed to work in government or in a place that made him rich. They lived in a big house and had two vehicles. Their home was very nice. They looked rich.

They had a section of the living room designated as a library with a lot of books – more books than I have seen in my whole life. As soon as we settled down, I went to the library and started working through the books. Initially, I could not find ones that I could read. After a few days in Aunt Sarah's house, I was able to find some of the books that I could read. I would go to the library to read anytime I am not doing any chores.

I did not smell the rat coming. I only had the awful requirement of being upbraided often by my aunt's husband for what I had done to bring such calamity to my parents. It made me ashamed and unhappy each time I had to stand before him and listen to how evil I was.

At first, I never suspected anything when he called me to stand before him and hear how bad I was. Then, he started calling me to remind me about my awful past when no one else was around.

One day, I observed that while I stood before him, he eyed me in a way that made me very uncomfortable. I noticed that his eyes were settled on my growing breasts. I had scanty clothing most of the time, and I could feel him trying to look through my armpit to see my breasts.

The extent of my trauma is such that I am still in a state of confusion. I was not able, in those days, to fathom anything. I did not see it coming, and so I did not plan a reaction.

One day, he called me. While I feared that I was going to take another bashing for my evil, he surprised me by asking me to go and boil water for him to take his bath and make tea.

"Your aunt has gone for a meeting at the church and will not be returning until late in the evening," he said.

I did not see how such information was relevant to me at that time.

When I informed him that the water had boiled, he asked me to prepare the one for his bath and take it to the bathroom in their bedroom. I had never had a reason to be in their bedroom before. I helped with cleaning the house, but my work was limited to the kitchen and the compound outside. A housekeeper came on some days of the week to clean the whole building.

My brother James was still asleep that morning. He had a rough night and could not sleep for a long time. It was only at dawn that he finally fell asleep.

As I took the water into the bathroom, I noticed that their bedroom was big, with a huge, well-made bed. The room smelled fresh and nice. As soon as I placed the water in the bathroom, my aunt's husband followed behind me. When I felt someone behind me, I turned and saw him stark naked with an erect penis.

I made to run, but he blocked me and locked the door. The water I was carrying fell from my hands and spilled on the ground. I started crying and pleading with him to leave me alone. He did not listen. He quickly grabbed me, tore off my dress, and started sucking my small, pointed breasts. I continued to plead, to kick at him, and to cry. All of this fell on deaf ears.

Though he was older than my father, he was quite strong. He kept sucking my breasts until I became weak and started feeling wet in my vagina. It seemed he noticed because he put his finger inside me and said, "You are even ready."

He opened the bathroom door and took me to his bed. He laid me on their matrimonial bed and said that I should cooperate with him so that he would take care of me.

"The first time a man did what you are doing now, he died, and my father went to prison. And you have said it yourself that I am evil. You would be bringing evil on yourself oooo!" I said to him, hoping in vain to dissuade him.

"This time around, it is you that will suffer alone," he said.

He pinned me to the bed, and despite the horror on my face, he tore off my pants and tried to force his big penis into my small vagina. He struggled without success. Suddenly, he started quaking. Then, some milky substance, which I now know to be sperm, started spilling out of his penis.

When he stopped quaking and the spilling stopped, he fell off my body with a relaxed look on his face. I picked up my torn panties and used them to wipe off the sperm all over my pubic area, vagina, and thighs. I used the panties to cover my vagina while I ran out of the bedroom into my own room and cried for most of the day.

After a long while, he came to my room, now dressed. He had taken his bath and dressed back as the 'honorable' man I had once thought he was. Now, I saw him as the most dishonorable man on earth. He threw my torn dress in my direction and said, "Don't worry, I will buy you more dresses and pants, you hear?"

He then warned, "Your aunt must not hear about this! If she does, you will be out in the street with nobody to care for you. If you behave well, I will take care of you. I will send you back to school."

I continued to mourn my lot. I am sure I became listless. My aunt noticed and asked what was wrong. I lied that I had a headache. She gave me painkillers and told me that if I felt feverish, I should let her know so I could treat malaria or go to the hospital. I thanked her, took some water, and pretended to take the tablets, but I threw them away.

My aunt's husband took every opportunity he could to warn me to stay quiet and not tell my aunt anything. He promised he would take care of me and make sure I lacked nothing.

As he promised, he bought me some dresses and pants. I told him I did not want them. He insisted that I should have them. I asked him, "When I wear the dresses, who will I tell my aunt bought them for me?"

He said I should only wear them when my aunt traveled, but that I could wear the pants all the time.

It seemed he decided to woo me instead of forcing me. He continued to buy me pants and anything he considered good for me and James, my brother. James started getting attached to him. Anytime the family sat together—family now consisting of my aunt, her husband, James, and me, as his two children did not live at home—he would throw glances at me. I did my best to conceal any connection between the two of us.

As he bestowed more and more gifts upon me, I became increasingly relaxed with his advances. He would chase me with his eyes when others were in the house, and when no one was around, he would find ways to touch my buttocks as if by accident. When the house was empty, I feared he would come for me, but to my surprise, he would not. Instead, he behaved like a small boy infatuated with me.

He soon found a way to buy me things with my aunt's knowledge. One day, while we were all seated in the living room, he told my aunt that he had seen some nice shorts and canvas shoes that would be good for James while he was out buying stockings. He dropped a hint that the next time he was there, he would buy them for James. A week later, he brought James two pairs of shorts, two colorful canvas shoes, stockings, and two T-shirts. He also brought an additional T-shirt and gave it to his wife to give to me, saying that he had seen it in the shop while buying for James but wasn't sure if it would fit me. My unsuspecting aunt brought the T-shirt to me. It was nice, and I really liked it.

A month or so later, my aunt traveled to Ondo Town, where they were from. While she was away, he went shopping for me. He called me into the living room and handed me a bag full of dresses, deodorant, soap, body cream, hair cream, and body spray. He said he wanted me to bathe at least twice a day and apply the deodorant, perfume, and creams after bathing.

When I hesitated to accept the items, he told me to take them and that if I behaved well, he would convince my aunt to send me back to school and ensure I had a great life. That felt alright in my heart. He asked me to go take a bath, apply the cream, perfume, and deodorant, wear one of the new dresses and pants, and return so he could see.

I took my time bathing. I wanted to offer myself to him—to pay him back for all he had done for me. And he no longer taunted me with my misfortune. I applied the cream generously to both my hair and body. Then, I used the deodorant and sprayed perfume on my dress and parts of my body, just as I had seen in a movie once.

I liked what I saw in the mirror after I finished dressing.

My aunt's husband was also fond of putting on movies where people kissed, held hands, and had sex. They all seemed happy doing it. I secretly hoped that one day, I would be happy like them when I had sex.

James had started getting hooked on TV. He was so excited about cartoons. My aunt's husband had it all planned. He tuned the television to a cartoon station, called both of us to come and watch, and when he saw that James was engrossed, he gave me a wink and left for his bedroom.

After some time, I went to the kitchen, used a side door, and went to his room. He was so happy to see me. He opened his arms, and I ran into them, feeling at home. All my fears were gone.

He apologized for the first day we met. He told me he had "fallen in love" with me the first day I arrived at their home. *Love, infatuation, sexual desire—I did not really understand those words, and even today, they all seem to mean the same to me.* He apologized for taunting me before and said he had just been childish when what he really wanted was to have me.

I asked about my aunt, and he said that she was a great woman but that the best thing for us was to make sure she never found out.

In an uncanny way, I felt good about the scheme.

He kissed me, and I responded. Unlike the hell that my two previous experiences had been, this was ecstatic. I wanted more and more of his kisses. It was so cool. I laid my head on his chest and dreamed about having the whole world.

His caresses were beyond my imagination. In moments, I was fully wet, yearning for real, penetrative sex. I hoped to enjoy it just like the women in the movies, who always seemed happy during sex.

He used only his hands to ignite a fire in my body. I started tearing at his pajamas, which he had put on in anticipation of my arrival. He noticed my yearning and helped me out of my new, fresh dress and pants.

He said, "We need to be gentle so that it won't be painful and so I can enter you properly."

He was careful. Since I was already wet, and his own semen was pouring, the penetration was only slightly painful. To my sweet horror, his rather large penis went all the way inside me. I felt as if he might break my bones—it seemed to reach the very end of my small body, as if it were touching my spine.

He took his time, working on me until I quaked and released my juices. I gripped him as if my life depended on holding him. That seemed to loosen my vagina, allowing him to move faster until he gave out a yell, gripping and squeezing me as if he wanted to wring the life out of me.

When he finished, we both fell asleep in each other's arms. It took James calling for me to wake us up. I jumped out of bed, dressed quickly, took my detour, and went to join him. The TV had blanked out due to a network problem, and I assured him it would come back. Then, I went into our room and continued sleeping.

While my aunt, her husband, and I lived like husband and wives, we had sex almost every day—and I enjoyed it.

About this time, I was barely thirteen years. We continued to play our game for more than one year. From time to time, I would wonder about my aunt and how all this would be happening under her nose without her knowing. My mother would have smelt rat long ago.

As he promised, he worked with my aunty to help me go back to school, and James was registered in primary school too.

I later learned that my aunt's husband had retired from service. My aunty was running her business, which was the mainstay of the family, though the old man received his pension. As he told me, some of his investments also yielded money from time to time. However, my aunt's business seemed to be thriving, requiring her attention constantly.

About two years into this sin, one of my aunt's sons came home for the holidays. The moment he saw me, he came after me like a bee to a flower. When I told him that we were supposed to be relatives, he was disappointed. But then he came back and said we should do it in secret.

What a dilemma. What was I to do in this kind of situation? Though I found him attractive, I felt it would be one evil too many. I wondered how the old man would take it.

Since my old man's son came back, we had not been able to rendezvous. All our efforts failed because he was at home most of the time or had friends visiting. He had been abroad for more than three years without coming home, so he was savoring every opportunity of his brief stay.

In our desperation to have some fling, we quickly rushed into the bedroom one afternoon when we thought everyone had gone out and James was immersed in his cartoon movies. We were in such a hurry that we didn't remember to lock the bedroom door.

We practically threw our clothes off as we rushed to steal a quick moment before Gbenga returned home. The old man had just penetrated me, and as soon as I let out a yell of pleasure, we saw the door swing open. There stood Gbenga, petrified at the door, the word "Pa" hanging unfinished in his mouth.

I grabbed the bedspread to cover myself while the old man scrambled to gather his trousers and shirt around his groin. Stammering, he said, "Gbenga, please, just tell me anything… anything… you… you nee… nee… need, and I will do it for you."

Gbenga stormed out of the room as soon as he gathered himself. I quickly pulled my gown over my head, grabbed my underwear in my hands, and ran out.

The old man dressed up, came out, and started calling for Gbenga. He followed him all the way to his room, where he found him pacing back and forth. Kneeling, the old man begged him for forgiveness.

"Please, ask for anything to compensate you for the embarrassment I have caused you," he pleaded.

Gbenga didn't say a word. The old man then promised to give him $7,000 to enable him to purchase a car when he returned to the USA. Still, Gbenga remained silent.

When he finally spoke, his voice was firm.

"Pa, you know that was dirty, what you did. Right under your own roof and on the bed you'll share with your wife tonight? And this girl is just a baby. Weren't you supposed to be raising her up?"

"Yes, Gbenga, you are right," the old man admitted. "But you must forgive me. Please promise not to tell your mom—this could kill her. I don't know what came over me."

Gbenga sighed. "Okay. Man to man. But sin no more."

I listened from the door that separated Gbenga's room from the one where I slept with James. I thought it was over.

That day passed.

The next night, I heard a tap on the door between my room and Gbenga's.

"Sarah, open the door. It's me, Gbenga," he whispered.

"Gbenga, what's the problem? Are you alright?" I asked.

"Yes, Sarah. We need to talk about what happened yesterday."

"Gbenga, please… forgive us," I pleaded.

"Yes, I have forgiven you, Sarah. That's why I want us to talk about it. If I hadn't forgiven you, you know what should be happening now, don't you?" he said.

My thoughts raced in different directions, but I couldn't make sense of what he was after.

"Okay, Gbenga, but you'll have to come through the front door because this door between us is nailed shut."

"Alright. Open the locks, and I'll dash in as quickly as I can through the front," he whispered.

I heaved a sigh—of tension rather than relief. Quietly, I climbed down from the bed and unlatched the door. Quickly, Gbenga slipped in as if ensuring no one saw him.

"Wow! I can see what drove the old man crazy. You are so beautiful, cute, and irresistible," he said, attempting to hold me.

I stepped aside. "What can I do for you, Gbenga?" I asked with a hint of indignation, though I concealed it behind a small smile. I felt I had to smile to avoid making him angry.

"You know, I've been eyeing you since I got here. I even asked you to be my 'lover,' and you refused, claiming we are relatives. Now I know why—you refused me because of the old man. But now that I've caught you with my father, I don't care about the whole 'we're related' thing anymore. What you two did is worse than anything I could do with a relative. So, I want you. Let's go to my room and do it," Gbenga said.

"Gbenga, please…" I pleaded.

"Sarah, don't 'Gbenga, please' me. It's either you play, or your little game with the old man is up."

"But… you promised your father you had forgiven him?"

"When did I do that?" he asked.

"I overheard your conversation with him yesterday," I said.

"Well, for your information, the only reason I forgave him was so I could have you—without him being able to stop me."

"Gbenga, if we were not related, I wouldn't mind," I said, trying to sound matter-of-fact.

"Well, young lady, I don't care about the relation 'thing.' You either play, or your game with the old man is up."

Tears started rolling down my cheeks. I began sobbing and dropped to my knees to beg him.

He knelt with me, enfolded me in his arms, and said, "It's not the worst thing in the world. It's not as if I'm just demanding sex from you to cover up for you. If you remember, I desired you from the first day we met, and as soon as I settled down, I asked you to be my girlfriend."

He rocked me until I stopped crying. He gazed straight into my eyes and said, "You deserve more than you're getting. I'll leave you now. Think about my proposal for friendship. Think about the fact that I would be unhappy if you rejected me. I will call on you tomorrow to hear what you've decided."

"Wow! What an escape," I thought.

But as he left, I couldn't get him out of my mind. I thought about him. I felt that I really liked him—though not to the point of engaging in a sexual relationship with him. After all, he is my cousin. In our culture, I'm told, close relatives like us do not marry each other.

Regardless of what logic I worked through my mind, I couldn't stop thinking about him. I thought of how dangerous it would be to have an angry, desiring man in the same house, especially given the illicit affair I had with his father. All sorts of unnerving thoughts filled my heart and mind until I didn't even know when I fell asleep.

I didn't see much of Gbenga all day. As I was getting ready for bed, I heard movement in his room. He seemed to have come home late that night. All my efforts to sleep were futile as I kept wondering if he would come to ask for my decision. I hadn't decided anything, and I would never, of my own volition, choose to have a sexual relationship with him, given our relationship and the dirty, complicated affair with his father. I also feared what would happen if he felt unhappy with my refusal. I was struggling with all these thoughts when I heard a gentle tap on the connecting door.

"Sarah, my baby, have you decided?"

My heart skipped.

"Ah! Gbenga, I was praying you would forget me."

"Well, Sarah, my baby, your prayers weren't answered."

I didn't say a word. My mind was now running riot. What do I do? What do I say?

There was a long silence. After what seemed like an eternity, Gbenga said, "Well, Sarah, I need you. But I won't force you. I won't report your misbehavior to Mom. But I need you."

Dilemma!

What is happening to me? What is this life? What is this lot of mine?

While I was deep in these thoughts, I heard a light, almost shy knock at the door. I got up and opened it. Gbenga came in, dressed in his pajamas and white room slippers. He looked so handsome. He opened his arms, gesturing for me to fall into them and hug him. And that's exactly what I did.

He held me tight—so tight that his body pressed hard against my breasts, which had enlarged in the last few months, with thick nipples that I was proud to admire. His pressure sent shivers all over my body. I clung to him like I didn't want to let go. His penis became hard and pressed against my stomach. He had no pants on. I could feel its warmth through the pajamas.

We started kissing.

James, who was asleep, stirred. We came to our senses and stopped. We watched him turn over and continue sleeping.

"Let's go to my room," Gbenga whispered.

"What about your parents? Aren't they in the living room?" I whispered back.

"No, they've gone to bed," he whispered.

I grabbed a wrapper and wrapped it around my nightie, which was quite revealing and short. We tiptoed to his room. He barely closed the door before grabbing my hand, pulling me close, and planting a kiss on my forehead. Then he swept me off my feet, pressed me against his body, and laid me on his bed.

My nightgown was one of those sexy ones that Gbenga's father had bought for me. It was a sleeveless dress with a rope tied in a double bow at the middle, easily undone with a single pull. He pulled the rope, and the nightie fell apart, leaving my small, cute body exposed, beckoning him to take me. I had no panties on.

He frantically started pulling off his two-piece pajamas. When he finally managed to remove them, he came down on me hard. His thrusts were aimless—most of them landed on my thighs and the edge of my vagina, causing pain and injury. Before I knew it, he came. He started breathing fast and poured his sperm all over my body.

He rolled away from me and buried his face in the pillow. For a moment, I didn't know what was happening. Then I heard sobs.

"Gbenga, what is it?" I asked.

Through his sobs, he said, "I have a problem with premature ejaculation. I don't know what to do. It's ruining my life."

I was at a loss for how to deal with this kind of situation.

What is premature ejaculation? I asked myself.

Here is a sophisticated, American-returned man. What do I know? All I know about sex was forced upon me. I was only just beginning to enjoy sexual intercourse with old Gbenga's father, largely because he took his time to coach me and make me enjoy it. What could I possibly teach Gbenga about sex? I kept asking myself.

In my dilemma, all I could remember to do was say, "Gbenga, maybe it is because I am small, and you are doing it for the first time with me. Let's go and clean up and try again. I think it will work next time we try."

I stretched my hand to hold him, and he rolled into my small body as if he were a baby I had to care for. I felt that he was depending on me. That both emboldened me and worried me. Still, I decided to apply all the lessons I had learned from the old man when we had sex.

He went into the bathroom and fetched water in a small bucket. He brought his hand towel, soaked it in water, pressed the water out, and started cleaning his body. I took the towel from him and, while using my left hand to squeeze his right hand, gently cleaned him up. When I finished wiping off the sperm he had poured all over his body, I soaked the towel back in the water, washed it off, and cleaned myself up.

I dropped the towel back into the bucket, went to his dresser, and picked up a body spray that I saw there. I sprayed it on my laps, my armpits, and my neck, then did the same for him. Kneeling in front of him, I started sniffing the body spray on his thighs. Then I kissed him, moving from his lap up to his chest. I pushed at him gently, and he got the message, sitting down on the bed.

I sat on his lap and kissed him hard on the lips. He responded, and as I nudged him, he fell onto his back. Now on top of him, I kissed him, and his penis became erect again. I took it, put it into my vagina, sat on it, and started working on him. Before long, he joined in the rhythm. His penis was not as long as his father's, but the position I adopted ensured it touched the edge of my womb, giving me both pain and pleasure.

After a while, he screamed and held me so tightly that I later found his nails had cut into my skin. He poured his sperm inside me and held me until we both fell asleep.

When we woke up, he picked me up in his arms, kissed my vagina, and thanked me for giving him his first real taste of sex.

"I have been a devastated man. All my previous efforts to have sex with both Black and white girls in America ended in disaster. My premature ejaculation was the killer. Once it happened, the girls would tell me off—some even mocked me. Nobody ever picked me up, dusted me off, and restored me. You are the only one."

He fell back into my small hands and body and slept again.

We were startled awake when Gbenga's mother entered the living room, switched on the lights, and went into the kitchen. Gbenga sneaked out to check on her. Once he saw she was out of sight, he returned and told me to run for it. I tiptoed back to my room, lay on the bed, and processed everything that had happened.

I was elated, though—that small me could be the restorer of a man's faith and hope in himself.

Gbenga sang all day. He never left to see anyone outside the home. For two days in a row, he did not go out. His mother wondered aloud why he wasn't visiting friends or having them visit him. He sang, whistled, and hummed all the music he knew. Whenever he could, he would sneak into my room, hug me, thank me, and rush out again.

However, the more I tried to extend my dreams beyond Gbenga or his father, the more I felt a foreboding sense that what we were doing was not right—that it would never end well. But I did not know what to do. Most of the time, I ended up feeling trapped in a dilemma, imprisoned by walls I could not escape until they exploded over my head.

Any time I reflected on my situation, I was left with the disturbing feeling that life was not fair. Was there no other way to live this life—to have family, fulfilling sex, peace of mind, and happiness, just like I had with my mother, father, and James before the day Tunde raped me?

Why did I have to live like this? I asked myself many times, but no answers ever came.

Before the bubble burst, I saw less and less of Gbenga's father. But we still managed one or two flings when no one was home or when my aunt traveled and Gbenga went to visit a friend.

With Gbenga, we had sex almost every night. One day, when his parents were out, he came into my room and removed the nails securing the door between us. When he wanted me, he would simply tap. I would make sure James was asleep, unlatch the door, and climb onto Gbenga's bed, where his outstretched arms were waiting.

He insisted I lead in our sexual encounters, hoping it would help keep his premature ejaculation in check. Many times, I succeeded in managing his buildup and delaying his release, and he was elated beyond measure.

He even started suggesting that we run away, get married, and never come back if they condemned us for marrying each other.

When it was time for Gbenga to return to the USA, he hesitated. He could not bring up the issue with his parents. He asked me to stay in their house, promising to go to the USA, make plans, and come back for me after he finished his education.

I did not put much hope in his promise or plan. Though it was fun being with him, especially having control over him, the thought of what we were doing often made me ashamed. I also suspected that when he was ready to marry, he would remember that I had been a rotten child, sleeping with his father, and never consider me worthy of being his wife.

I was glad when he left. Managing both father and son was difficult. All the sneaking around was too much for me.

A few weeks after Gbenga left, I started feeling sick. My menstrual cycle, which had only recently begun, became irregular, coming only when it wanted to. Before I started feeling sick, I had already wondered why my period had not come in some time.

Then fever, vomiting, and an overwhelming sense of sickness took hold. I told my aunt, "I am sick. I have a headache, cold, and catarrh."

"It must be malaria," she said, giving me pain relief tablets. "I will take you to the hospital when I return from business today."

That evening, when she returned, she asked if I had bathed and eaten. To both questions, I answered yes.

She grabbed her bag and took me to the hospital.

When I met the doctor, the first thing he asked was, "When did you last have your period?"

"I can't remember. It's never regular," I said.

He examined my eyes, lips, blood pressure, palms, and fingernails.

Then he wrote something on a paper, rang the bell, and a nurse came in. Handing her the paper, he stood up and asked me to follow her. The nurse took me to the lab, where they collected my blood and urine samples.

When I returned with the nurse to his office, he stood up and walked me to my aunt.

"What is wrong with her, doctor? What medicine are you prescribing for her?" my aunt asked.

"I want her to undergo some tests before we begin treatment to ensure there are no mistakes. Meanwhile, give her pain-relieving tablets and vitamin C."

My aunt took the prescription from the doctor, and we went to the pharmacy to obtain the medication.

The next evening, my aunt and I returned to the hospital to collect the results and, hopefully, receive treatment. When we met the doctor, he pulled out my file, took an envelope, and handed it to my aunt.

"Your daughter is five months pregnant, Mrs. Adeleke."

My aunt's mouth opened as if she wanted to say something. Her hand remained stretched out to take the paper. Then she muttered some unintelligible words, suddenly slumped into the chair, and passed out.

"Nurse! Nurse!" the doctor called.

When the nurse arrived with another hospital staff member, they carried my aunt and placed her on the doctor's outpatient bed.

The doctor examined her with his stethoscope and said, "She is in a coma." He wrote something on a piece of paper, tore it out, and gave it to the nurse. Shortly after, the nurse returned with an IV drip, mounted it, and set it up for my aunt.

In the commotion, I didn't even think about what the doctor had said—about being pregnant for five months.

When the drip had been set up and the nurse left the room, the realization suddenly surged into my mind.

"Pregnant? Doctor, did you say I am pregnant?"

"Yes, little woman, you are pregnant. You are five months along. We must find a way to help you carry it through. And you are just a baby," he said with empathy, shaking his head.

"Ahhh! What a world! Ahhhhh! What a world!" was all I could say.

Mr. Israel Adeleke, my aunt's husband, had been summoned by the doctor. He arranged for my aunt to be moved to a private ward.

"Sarah, what happened to your aunt?" Mr. Adeleke—my aunt's husband and my secret abuser—asked.

"The doctor gave her a letter and told her I was five months pregnant," I said, tears streaming down my face. "She fainted."

"How can you get pregnant? You are just a kid! Oh my God, what have I done?"

"Em! Em! Em! You cannot call my name, ooo! Do you hear me, Sarah? You cannot call my name, oooo!" he repeated. "If you dare, you are dead. My wife would not choose you over me. You will be out there like a vagabond. After the commotion dies down, we will find a way to handle it. Do you hear me?"

I kept crying, not knowing what to do or what would become of me. It flashed in my mind that my days in this beautiful home were over. And this, despite succumbing to the sexual demands of my aunt's husband, who had made it clear that my stay in his house depended on being his sex slave.

Later that night, my aunt woke up.

"What happened? What am I doing here in a hospital bed? Where is Sarah? How is she? She was sick, and I brought her to the hospital."

"You fainted," her husband replied.

"Where is Sarah?"

"That rotten girl? She is here!"

"Ah! Israel, do not talk about the little girl like that in her presence!"

I had never heard my aunt call her husband by his first name before. I didn't even know his name was Israel.

"Why not? Did you not hear what the doctor said? She is pregnant. How could she put herself in that kind of mess?"

"Aha! Sarrrrah! Pregnant?! Who put you belle? You 'don' kill your parents. You want to kill me too. Who put you belle?"

I kept crying. This time, I cried louder. My aunt continued shouting. Her husband tried to stop her, but she would not be appeased. She continued shouting:

"Who put you belle?! Who put you belle?!"

She started struggling to get up. I cried even louder. Then the doctor walked in.

"Ah! Mr. Adeleke, you are here. Okay then, madam is awake. I believe this is a matter better handled at home than in the hospital. But remember, she is five months along. Abortion is not advised."

My aunt was discharged, and we all left in Mr. Adeleke's car. My aunt and I continued crying all the way home.

I didn't know what to feel.

Another old man had taken advantage of my vulnerabilities, and yet I was the one being blamed. What kind of fate was this? I wondered.

But more than that, I was confused—too overwhelmed to even process my predicament. I sat in the car, my mouth open, until we reached home.

When we arrived, my aunt struggled to get out of the car. She immediately sank onto the sofa in the sitting room, and her husband joined her.

The moment I entered the room, she got up and grabbed me.

"So, Sarah, they sent you to come and kill me!" she screamed, pummeling me with anything she could grab.

"Now, foolish girl, tell me—who put you belle?!"

Mr. Adeleke just sat there, saying nothing. When I looked at him from the corner of my eye, he realized I was looking to him for help. He tightened his lips—a silent warning not to say a word.

But my aunt wouldn't relent in her beating. I kept crying helplessly. She only stopped when blood started coming from my mouth and nose.

Finally, after over five minutes of continuous beating, Mr. Adeleke spoke.

"Sarah, you have to stop! You will kill the little girl. And your own health is not good. Please, Sarah, stop—please."

"Nooo! She has already killed me! We are going to die together tonight! She must tell me who put her belle!"

"Haaa! I am worried about you. Some things are better left unsaid for one's health."

"I do not understand you, Israel!"

"I have said my own, ooo," he muttered.

He waited briefly, then stood up and left the sitting room.

My aunt resumed her onslaught.

"If you don't want to talk in life, you will talk in death! I will kill you with my own hands, since your mission in this family is to destroy us! You have ruined your parents. Your father is in prison, and your mother is now mad—all because of you!"

The commotion must have woken my brother, James. He came out and joined me in crying.

At this point, my aunt went for my throat. She choked me until I was gasping for breath.

"I will tell! I will tell!"

"Oya! Start telling me."

She loosened her grip on my throat just a little.

"It is Daddy and Gbenga, ooooo."

"Oti o! W-who?"

She suddenly let go of me, and both of us fell to the floor. I knocked over the center table and tumbled onto James. In her fall, she hit her head on the edge of the sofa's armrest. She gasped and passed out.

I screamed even louder.

Mr. Adeleke rushed out of the room. "What happened? What happened?" he kept asking. Nobody was in the right state of mind to provide any answers.

He picked up his wife and screamed, "Oh my God! What have I done?"

He panicked, running back and forth between the bedroom and outside. Moments later, he reentered the sitting room and started dragging his wife outside.

James and I cried all night. I did not see Mr. Adeleke again that night.

The next morning, he returned to the house and asked me, "Can you boil water, put it in the flask, and pack a basket with the chocolate drink, milk, some biscuits, and fruits from the fridge?"

I managed to drag myself up from the floor where James and I had spent the night. I pulled myself together, boiled the water, and packed the food flask and basket. I used the opportunity to prepare James for school and walked him to the nearby school before leaving with my aunt's husband for the hospital.

"What happened to your aunt?" he asked.

"When she was about to choke me to death, I had to tell her that it is you and Gbenga who have been sleeping with me," I said.

"Oti o! Gbenga did what?"

"Gbenga told me that he forgave you on the condition that I would agree to do the same thing with him that I was doing with you. Otherwise, the deal was off. We had to remove the nail from the door between our rooms so we could sneak in and out without being noticed."

"You told me everything would be alright if I agreed. I warned you that the first man who did this to me was killed by my father, and my father was imprisoned while my mother went mad. You called me an evil child, yet you took pleasure in pouring filth onto my stolen innocence. And now, what do we have?" I lamented.

"Ah! This world. Ah! This world."

Mr. Adeleke was dumbfounded. He just stared at me in confusion. It was obvious he had no idea what to say or do.

My aunt was in a coma for six days. When she finally woke up, I was at the hospital with her husband. The moment she saw me, she started crying.

She turned to me and said, "I do not want to see you in my house if I return with my two legs. You evil witch! You have ruined your family, and now you have ruined mine. God must punish you! Disappear from my presence right this minute. I do not want to see you ever again."

All of Mr. Adeleke's efforts to calm her down failed.

I left the hospital immediately and ran home. I packed my belongings—but only the things my aunt had bought for me. I left behind everything Mr. Adeleke had given me.

In my mind, I felt that those gifts—used to make our immorality seem normal—might haunt me for the rest of my life if I kept them. Those gifts had once meant so much to me. I desired them, welcomed them as rewards for sleeping with him, for having sex with him each time his wife—my aunt—was not home.

I left my aunt's house without knowing where to go. I just kept walking. I had no destination, no plan. Before long, darkness fell.

While wandering through a dark alley, two boys attacked me. They snatched my bag, probably thinking it held something valuable. That incident terrified me. I stopped walking and felt completely exposed.

Retracing my steps, I spotted an empty shed that looked like a stall for selling food. Nearby, there was a compound with people's voices coming from inside. I slipped into the shed and waited, hoping to stay there until morning before continuing my journey to nowhere.

I must have fallen asleep.

A voice startled me awake.

"Wake up, young woman. This is not a safe place for someone like you. What are you doing here?"

"Please, I just want to sleep until morning," I pleaded. "Please allow me, Ma."

"What is the problem? Would you mind sharing with me? A problem shared is a problem half solved, they say."

"You don't want to hear my story, madam. If you knew me, you would do best to leave me alone," I said.

"Well, young lady, whether you talk to me or not, you need to leave this place. You could be robbed or raped here. Very soon, bad people will start combing this area for victims. Come with me. Tomorrow, you can continue wherever you are going."

"Okay, Ma. Thank you," I said.

I followed her home. She lived in the compound behind the shed. She told me she was a nurse and had just returned from her afternoon duty when she noticed me.

"What are you running from?" she asked.

"Ah! It is unspeakable. My life has been one big mess after another, beginning at age eleven. Now I am pregnant by either a man or his son—I do not know which one. All I know is that both forced me into sex because I was a helpless refugee in their home.

I was raped by a neighbor when I was eleven. Out of anger, my father killed the man. He went to prison, and my mother lost her mind. My father's older sister took in my younger brother and me. From the first day I arrived at her house, the old man—my aunt's husband—made my life miserable. He ultimately attacked and raped me.

When he was done, he warned me that if I told my aunt, I would be out on the street. I hid it from her. Later, he started buying me gifts and convinced me to sleep with him in exchange for sending my brother and me to school. I agreed.

We had been involved for almost a year when his son returned from America. He caught us in the act. His father begged for forgiveness, and the son agreed. But later, he came to me and said that he only forgave his father so he could have the same thing with me. If I refused, he would expose everything to his mother.

I became the sex slave of both father and son. The young man left for America only two weeks ago. I became sick, and the doctor told me I was five months pregnant."

My aunt had a heart attack, and when she woke up paralyzed, she swore to kill me if I waited for her to come back from the hospital.

I discovered that the nurse looked happy when she heard that I was pregnant. There was a glow on her face that I could not explain, as I expected her to be in sorrow for me.

"Young woman, relax. It is God that brought you here. I will take care of you and your baby. I am a nurse. Tomorrow, I will take you to the hospital and register you. Go to the kitchen, boil some water, and take your bath. I will prepare us food. I know you must be hungry."

I eyed her with suspicion. Then I asked, "You are not a man; how will I pay you back?"

"It is not written that every gift you get must be repaid. Don't worry yourself."

"Well, life has shown me that there is always a price tag. Ever since I caused our parents to lose our simple but happy family life and our home, I have had to pay for everything I got with my body."

"Don't worry your little head, girl. Everything will be alright."

My mind never settled on the idea that everything was alright with this woman. Things were happening too nicely and too fast for me to believe that everything was fine—or ever would be.

The next day, I went to the hospital with her. There was something unsettling about the place. It was tucked away in a dark alley with no signpost. Unless you were inside, there was no indication that it was a hospital. Even inside, it looked and smelled more like a slaughterhouse than a medical facility.

During the antenatal class, I observed that everyone around me was a little girl about my age or slightly older. There were only a few who appeared to be between eighteen and twenty years old. In total, we were about fifteen to twenty young, pregnant girls in the class.

I noticed that no husband ever brought any of them to the hospital.

I was registered. I thought I overheard the "doctor" having a subdued argument with the nurse who brought me, discussing where I would stay. At least, I remember hearing the nurse say:

"Doctor, I am keeping this one with me. She is special."

"Nurse, I hope you have not started private practice. It could backfire, ooo," the doctor said.

"No, haa, doc-tor. This one na my relation, ooo," the nurse said, laughing as she came out.

I felt unsettled by that conversation and by the general nature of the hospital.

The kiosk where Nurse Eliza found me sleeping that night turned out to belong to her. She sold small groceries, food items, and condiments. She said she only opened it when she was not on duty. With my arrival, she asked if I was strong enough to run the shop every day. Once I regained my composure, I told her I could sell at the kiosk.

The next day, before she left for work, she brought out all her stock, and we displayed them on the table. She walked me through the prices and inventory. Over time, she added more items, and for as long as I was strong enough to manage the shop daily, business boomed.

One day, Nurse Eliza asked me, "What do you want to do after you give birth to your baby?"

"Honestly, Auntie Eliza, I do not know. I get the feeling that my life is ruined, and I am without hope. Where would I begin? I have lost everything I held dear—my father, my mother, and my little brother, James."

"To tell you the truth, sometimes I feel that it would be best if death came now to take me away."

"Stop talking like that, little woman. Don't you believe in God? He will make a way where there is no way."

That preaching made no sense to me. Though my parents took us to church from time to time, regular attendance was never a family standard. We went to church only when we woke up on the right side of the bed. The church had so many members that nobody cared if you were present or not. We merely appeared in clean—sometimes new—dresses to embrace the Sunday spirit.

"How would you like a big man and his wife to adopt your child, raise him or her for you, and maybe help you find a new, happy life?"

"How is that?" I asked.

"I have an uncle who is rich. He is married, but they do not have a child. If you are ready, I will tell them to come and adopt your baby when it is born. If it is a boy, they will be very happy with you. But even if it is a girl, they would still love to have a child. After all, they have not been able to have one of their own."

I had often wondered how I would cope with a child when I could barely cope with myself. So, the proposal sounded good to me.

"Well, Auntie Eliza, if your uncle and his wife would be happy to have the baby, I would be happy to give them the child. At least the baby might get a life that is not as rotten as mine. Thank you, Auntie Eliza."

A few days after this discussion, a man with a big vehicle came to the house with his wife. As soon as they reached the door, Auntie Eliza peeped through the window. Before opening the door, she hurried me into the bedroom and told me never to come out until they had left.

While inside, I overheard the following conversation:

"Nurse Eliza, you see, I want my wife to get the best care. I feel it would be best in the hospital. But she says she prefers private care. We have been struggling to have a baby of our own, and I do not want anything to happen to this pregnancy. Of course, I do not want anything to happen to my wife either. I hope you hear me well, because—"

"Ah! Mr. Afolabi, don't talk like that," Auntie Eliza interrupted. "There will be no problem. I am the main midwife in the hospital. Your wife doesn't need that crowd in the hospital. Besides, she needs special care."

"Darling, don't worry. Everything will be alright," the man's wife added.

"The truth is, I don't feel good about you not receiving care in a normal hospital… Well, Nurse Eliza, if anything goes wrong, you will not like what I will do. I don't care what it costs—I just want my wife to have a child, and for them to be safe."

"Don't worry, Mr. Afolabi. Nothing will go wrong, sir."

From that day on, Auntie Eliza treated me like a special jewel. She answered my every call, looked after me well, and made sure I never lacked food or clothing. In fact, at one point, I started feeling uncomfortable with her growing attentiveness.

From time to time, Nurse Eliza would brew some herbs and ask me to drink. Because it never tasted sweet enough for my liking, I always asked what it was and why I had to take it. She would always answer—

"Don't you see how you eat like a big cow? It would not be good if the child follows the way you are eating and grows too big for your small body and birth canal. That could be a disaster. I am preparing the baby to come out small so that you will be able to push it out through your small 'thing.' Or do you want us to tear your body before the baby comes out?"

"Ah! No, ooo. Thanks for your care, Mummy."

"You are welcome, my daughter."

It always made her happy when I addressed her as 'Mummy.'

Every two weeks, the man would bring his wife, drop her off, and leave. When the man arrived, Nurse Eliza would ask me to go into the bedroom. When he left, his wife would stay back. She looked heavy with pregnancy, but Nurse Eliza was not giving her any medicine. She would just sit and talk with Nurse Eliza.

Though she was supposedly in Nurse Eliza's house for special antenatal care, I never saw her take medicine or do the exercises that I and the other little women in the hospital were made to go through during our antenatal care. In the evening, her husband would return for her, and they would go home.

When we started doing weekly visits to the hospital, she also started coming to Nurse Eliza on a weekly basis. She continued this game—as I now understood it—until the day I was due.

When I became due, she fussed over me. She asked questions every now and then to know if labor had started. She told me about the signs I would see to indicate the onset of labor. She asked me to let her know as soon as I felt any of those signs.

"Auntie Eliza, this evening, I felt a lot of kicking, and my waist pained me so much. I could hardly move," I said.

"Oh, that is an early sign, ooo. If you feel any other sign tonight, wake me up and tell me. Do you hear?"

As soon as we finished this discussion about the early stage of my labor, she picked up her cell phone and went outside. She called someone. I only overheard her say, "Come quickly, she has started labor."

About an hour or so later, the man drove up with his wife to Nurse Eliza's house. Nurse Eliza rushed me into the bedroom and asked me to stay quiet. She said, "Even if you have any pain, endure it. I don't want to hear your voice."

"Em… em… I don't mean to be rude. It is good for you too, you hear? So please stay quiet," she retorted apologetically.

"Oh! My baby girl, sorry for my harsh words, you hear? I will come back soon to see how you are doing," she reassured.

Before you could finish spelling 'gorilla,' Nurse Eliza had transformed her living room into a labor room with light green-colored screens, a low hospital bed with light green-colored bedding, medical supplies, gloves, soaps, antiseptics, toiletries, and more. She moved the two upholstered chairs from the living room, along with her radio, TV, and some other furniture, into the kitchen.

Quickly, her small *I-pass-my-neighbor* generator came on. I did not believe it worked because it had not been used since she took me into her house almost four months earlier. We used electric light to watch TV and use the fan only when public electricity was available, which was occasional.

I looked through the window and saw him virtually carrying the woman as she appeared to be in serious labor. Nurse Eliza carried her box and another smaller bag into the house.

While I was inside the bedroom, the man brought his wife into the living-room-turned-labor-room. Nurse Eliza took control of the situation very well. I could hear her giving commands.

"Mr. Afolabi, be gentle with her, ooo! Put her on the maternity bed. Gently, sir. Aha!"

"What can I do to help, Nurse Eliza?" he asked.

"You will now go outside. I will examine her as soon as I wash my hands in the disinfected water and wear my gloves." That sounded like a performance, making sure Mr. Afolabi believed everything was in order.

"You don't think I should stay to help you in case you need to move her?"

"No, Mr. Afolabi. My assistants will be here soon. I have called them."

I was sure Nurse Eliza was putting on a show for Mr. Afolabi's attention. I suspected she was calculating that he was still nearby and probably listening, so she kept up the act.

"Madam, open your legs. Let me check if you are ready. Open them. Don't waste my time. When you were busy enjoying it with your husband, you did not cry *eeha eeha!*"

"Ah! You are not ready yet. Calm down, you hear."

"Em, Mr. Afolabi, your wife is not fully ready. You can go now. Come back tomorrow morning to check. Bring hot water for tea when you come."

"Wo! Nurse Eliza, I am staying right here, even if it means sleeping outside in the cold."

"If you sleep here, cold will not be your problem—it will be bad boys. If they see this big car of yours here, they will come again, thinking my brother from America has returned. The last time he came here, he left his car outside. Late at night, they came, beat us up, and took his car and all his American money."

"So please, Mr. Afolabi, go home. Your wife will be alright, you hear?" Nurse Eliza continued her act.

"Okay, Nurse Eliza, please take care of my wife. I am going."

"Not so fast, Mr. Afolabi. You can come in and greet your wife. Then leave some money with me for buying emergency things."

"Okay, let me come in to greet her. But she has enough money on her for anything she needs."

"Ah! Mr. Afolabi, you don't understand. When labor begins, your wife will not even remember where she kept her wedding ring. Leave some cash with me so we won't have to start calling and waiting for you when the need arises. Sometimes, it comes as an emergency."

"Okay, here is N20,000.00."

"Now you are talking. Go home, Mr. Afolabi. By this time tomorrow, you will be a proud father. Byyee."

"Bye, Nurse Eliza," he said.

"Iyawo mi! Stay strong for me, you hear? I love you," Mr. Afolabi said as he left the room.

"I love you too! Ooo! Eeha, eeha!" Mrs. Afolabi continued to exclaim.

I thought about the whole act; I did not initially understand it. But as soon as Mr. Afolabi left, his wife got up, sat on the bed, and started talking with Nurse Eliza as if she had never felt any pain in her life.

"Nurse Eliza, this thing must work ooo! I am beginning to be afraid," Mrs. Afolabi said worriedly.

"Don't worry your little head, woman. I have been in this business for more than five years now, and I have never had any problems. Just pray for the poor pregnant girl—that she will be able to deliver a living baby, whether she lives or dies."

"Amin! Amin! Amin!" Mrs. Afolabi echoed.

It was only then that it dawned on me—Mrs. Afolabi and Nurse Eliza were conspiring to deceive Mr. Afolabi. They had been pretending that Mrs. Afolabi was pregnant. The nurse was preparing me so that when I gave birth, she would hand over my baby to Mrs. Afolabi, making it seem as though she had given birth herself.

Well, I thought, they are wealthy. Maybe they would be a blessing for my child so that he or she would not come into my dreadful world. And look at me—what part of my body is capable of weaning a child at barely thirteen years old? The thought felt somewhat comforting.

I was in the middle of this thought when a sharp pang of pain seized me. I tried to muffle it, but realizing that Mr. Afolabi had gone, I let out a loud cry.

Nurse Eliza and Mrs. Afolabi rushed into the bedroom, where I was now writhing in pain on the floor. They picked me up and helped me to the living room, which had now been converted into a labor room. Gently, they laid me on a small bed.

Nurse Eliza put on a pair of gloves and said, "Let me examine her."

"My baby girl, don't worry. You will be okay soon. Auntie Eliza is here for you, okay?"

She then inserted her gloved hand into my vagina and worked her way inside.

"She is almost ready," she announced. "The water has broken, but the baby's head is not that close yet."

The pain continued to increase. It soon became too excruciating for me to bear, so I started crying loudly.

"Auntie Eliza, help me ooo! Auntie Eliza, help me ooo!" I continued to cry.

"My baby girl, don't worry. I am here with you," Nurse Eliza reassured me.

My pain worsened by the minute.

Nurse Eliza then checked the clock and examined me again.

"She is almost ready," she repeated.

By this time, two other women had arrived. They joined in helping me. One of them mopped the sweat that was running down my face and body like water.

"Undress her and give her the maternity cloth to wrap around her body," Nurse Eliza directed.

After what seemed like an eternity in pain—though it was probably just five to ten minutes—she announced, "Let me check her again."

"I think she is ready," Nurse Eliza reported. "Remove the maternity cover and get ready."

Mrs. Afolabi fussed around. "What now? What now?" she kept asking.

"Go into the bedroom and start praying. You know she is a little girl. It is only a fifty-fifty chance that she will make it—and the same for the baby," Nurse Eliza commanded her.

Mrs. Afolabi ran into the bedroom. And that was the last thing I remembered of that scene.

My pain became unbearable.

One of the women held my hands, and the other one held my legs, raising my knees. Nurse Eliza knelt between my legs.

"My baby, you are ready. When I tell you to push, you push as if you want to wee-wee or poo-poo, okay?"

All I could do was nod.

I thought about my life. I wanted to pray to die. Before I could begin the prayer, I heard a voice-like impression—"This is not the end of your life." I ended up saying, "Oh God, help me."

The pain became much stronger. I screamed.

"Stop screaming ooo. Otherwise, you will be screaming anytime you have to deliver a baby," one of the women scolded.

"My baby, you are ready. Now push with all your power," Nurse Eliza said.

I pushed and screamed at the same time.

"Continue, my baby! It is coming. Your God is awake. Puuuush!" Nurse Eliza encouraged me.

I pushed with all the energy in my body, mind, and heart. I even imagined the baby coming out, screaming at the same time.

I gripped the hand of one of the women tightly and pushed harder.

I noticed one of the women smiling. I felt a glimmer of hope and encouragement from that, so I pushed even harder until...

I must have passed out.

By the time I woke up, I had been cleaned up. The room was disinfected.

Mrs. Afolabi was now carrying a small bundle wrapped tightly, with a little red face peeking out. It was a boy!

For the first time in two or more years, I felt peace in my heart. Maybe I was just relieved that the pregnancy and labor pains were over. I couldn't quite explain it—it was something intrinsic.

Mrs. Afolabi was no longer carrying the heavy stomach of a pregnant woman. I watched her from the corner of my eye. She looked so happy.

I thought, *Well, my child, I will miss you every day of my life, and maybe one day, I will regret not raising you myself. But I feel that you will be cared for and raised by a woman who truly needs you.*

Once everything was cleaned and settled, Nurse Eliza called Mr. Afolabi.

"Mr. Afolabi! Mr. Afolabi! Hurry and come. Bring a goat and money to thank me. Your wife has been delivered of a baby boy!"

I felt a lump in my throat. I swallowed hard, but then I remembered my earlier thoughts about giving my baby a better life.

When Mr. Afolabi arrived, I was carried into the bedroom to hide.

After much excitement, celebration, and money being sprayed on Nurse Eliza and the other women, native songs in Yoruba filled the air.

Nurse Eliza and Mrs. Afolabi took care of me. They helped me heal both physically and emotionally.

Mrs. Afolabi visited as often as she could and always brought gifts.

During one of her visits, she and Nurse Eliza wanted to make sure I understood the terms of the transfer. They were probably afraid that I might cause trouble one day.

After delivering the gifts and asking about my well-being, they hesitated, unsure of who should speak first.

"Nurse Eliza, you should tell Sarah my worries," Mrs. Afolabi said.

"No, you should tell her what you are afraid of," Nurse Eliza responded.

Not sure what was wrong, I feared my son had died.

"Is my son alright, Mrs. Afolabi?" I asked.

"Oh yes, he is doing very well."

"Em! Em!" Mrs. Afolabi stammered.

Nurse Eliza spoke up. "My baby, what Mrs. Afolabi wants to tell you is that you must never try to see your baby or ask about him—so that her husband never finds out what happened. Do you understand?"

"I understand what you are asking, but that is hard and…"

"My baby," Nurse Eliza interrupted. "Remember when we talked about what would be best for your child and you? This is the best arrangement we can get. And Mrs. Afolabi will continue to be our friend and will help you from time to time."

"Yes, Sarah. We are all women. If you cover my shame, you will be in my heart forever."

"Okay, ma. Thank you for taking care of my baby. I cannot imagine what our life would be like without you being here for us. Thank you, Mrs. Afolabi. I pray that the boy will truly be your son. I pray that he will bring you joy. I am happy to have done one thing to make someone happy, for the first time in my miserable life, which has brought only calamity to those I love."

Tears flowed down my cheeks. Mrs. Afolabi's, too. She got up and hugged me. I felt like a woman in kinship with other women who faced different challenges in life, such as barrenness or childlessness.

That was the last time I saw Mrs. Afolabi. It was probably not her fault, as events disconnected me from Nurse Eliza, through whom I might have seen her again.

Nurse Eliza must have made a lot of money selling my son to the Afolabis in the ruse she and Mrs. Afolabi set up. She changed the color and furniture of her home. She changed her wardrobe and bought herself a small lady's motorcycle.

I continued selling at her grocery stand. The stock increased, and at least I had some kind of life. But I still missed my father. Some days, thoughts of my mother, brother, and father overwhelmed me, and I would sink into sorrow, often crying. Nurse Eliza would sometimes find me in that state and try to console me. Some nights, I woke up in tears, overcome by sadness.

The hormonal changes from pregnancy and childbirth made me grow—physically and emotionally—at the same time. Before long, young boys and men started hanging around Nurse Eliza's grocery stand, pretending to buy something while looking for a chance to chat with me.

But everything I had done with men had only brought me calamity. I wasn't taken in by their words. Their flattery, wooing, and games were easy to see through, and I stayed away from them.

One day, a man and a woman, probably his wife, arrived in a big car from the wealthier part of the city to visit Nurse Eliza. I was at the shop when they arrived. They asked if this was where Nurse Eliza lived, and I told them yes, pointing to her door. They spent some time with her before she escorted them out to their car, and they drove away.

That night, Nurse Eliza called me and asked what plans I had for myself. I told her I wasn't sure, but I hoped to return to school someday and finish my education. I also longed to know what had become of my brother James, my mother, and my father.

She philosophized, saying she liked to take life "one day at a time." Then she suggested that, if I didn't mind, she could help me get pregnant again. Another wealthy couple would adopt my child, and I would receive money to support myself.

I couldn't hide my shock at her shameless suggestion.

"Nurse Eliza! What do you take me for?" I asked, my annoyance obvious.

"Ah! Little woman, your voice is quite high. Forgive me, I did not mean to offend you. If you do not like the proposal, you can say so. I am only trying to let you know that you must be doing something serious if you wish to stay with me."

"So, what are you suggesting?"

"Well, little woman, there is another opportunity for you to get pregnant and give out your child for adoption—"

"Or for sale," I interrupted.

"Well, you have been nice to me. I cannot forget that in a hurry. But to become a prostitute and a tree bearing fruit for sale in the market—that is too much, Nurse…"

"For your information, young woman, if you are not going to cooperate, there will be no place for you here," she interjected.

"Other girls in your position live in dirty, crowded places and do this every year. Here, I have provided you with a home, good food, and nice clothes, and yet you refuse to cooperate. Many people are ready to take your place in this house."

I was stunned, to say the least. What had I walked into? Death was certainly better than the fate that had befallen me.

God, where are you? I thought I heard you say, 'It is not the end of my life.' What is this now? Is this 'the life?' I asked God.

"Auntie Eliza! You asked me not to pray for death, but your plan for me is worse than death. I cannot do this. What—"

She walked away, ending the conversation.

I wanted to ask her what would happen if I refused. I wanted her to say outright that I had to leave. Her words—"Many people are ready to take your place in this house"—made it clear, but perhaps I needed to hear her say it directly.

In the days that followed, Nurse Eliza became hostile. We used to have deep conversations about life and our experiences as women. Now, there was nothing. She came and went.

A week passed—no cooking in the house. Once we finished the food budget for the week, she made no further arrangements. I started starving. By the next week, I began taking biscuits from the grocery shop to survive.

One afternoon, she returned from work and found me crying. She simply said,

"You haven't even started. If you know what's good for you, obey me and carry a pregnancy for Chief Igbinoba and his wife. If you are not willing, then I am not willing to carry your burden."

"Auntie Eliza, you saved my life, and I am thankful. You made big promises when your uncle adopted my child. They took my son, and I have seen nothing. Now, you want me to become a prostitute—making and selling babies. I told you I felt it was better I was dead, and you promised me life. Is this the life you promised?"

"Little woman, so you are saying that I am a bad person, and you are good? You were the one who got yourself pregnant. I saved your life, and now you accuse me? Well, here is the reality—if you won't do this, you must leave my house."

"Nurse Eliza! I would rather die than choose to be a prostitute to survive and sell babies."

"Okay, little woman. You have made your choice. As you make your bed, so shall you lie on it. By noon tomorrow, I do not want to see you in my house again. Good night."

She left me in the living room, entered her bedroom, and shut the door. I sat there and cried all night. No solution came to my mind, but one thing was certain—I would not become a prostitute making and selling babies.

Early in the morning, I made up my mind. I bathed, gathered everything I owned—some clothes, two leather slippers, one rubber slipper, an extra set of earrings, and a wristwatch—and stuffed them into a small bag. I had N6,450.00 saved from the pocket money Nurse Eliza used to give me. I secured it in my gown pocket and set off.

I walked all day. I had no destination, no direction. I did not even know where I had been staying. I just kept moving. Whenever I grew tired, I rested under a tree or a shed.

I left the periphery of the city suburb that had been my home for the past year. I found myself in a busy, bustling city. There were too many people and vehicles. Everything moved too fast, and more than once, I was stunned by speeding cars that almost knocked me down. I saw a wide, seemingly endless road filled with yellow-painted buses moving rapidly. Several of them brushed past me, their drivers yelling and cursing.

I reached a place where many of the buses stopped to drop off and pick up passengers.

I overheard one of the conductors shouting, "Oshodi straight! Oshodi straight! Oshodi straight!"

I simply followed the crowd rushing toward the bus. I was practically pushed onto the big, long vehicle by the people behind me. I found a seat and sat down, clutching my small bag, which contained all my worldly treasures. The bus filled up quickly, with more people standing than sitting.

The huge, rickety truck-turned-bus lurched forward. Passengers hopped on and off even before the bus could come to a complete stop. Several others clung to the doors of the long yellow bus I was in, and many other reckless vehicles swerved through the crowded roads, filled with shouting and honking.

The wide road was packed with cars, buses, and people, forcing us to crawl along in what I later learned was called a "go-slow," meaning heavy, slow-moving traffic. I had no destination in mind— I just sat there.

Each time the conductor moved around collecting fares, I paid. I believe I paid more than three times. The fares were cheap, and I copied the others, handing the conductor ₦50 when I first saw others doing the same. He gave me ₦30 in change. The next time he came, I gave him ₦20. The third time, I handed him my last ₦10.

He shouted, "Wo! Wetin? Pay correct money!"

Flustered, I quickly took out my ₦100 note and gave it to him. He returned ₦80. So, the next time he came calling, I handed him ₦20 again.

I couldn't remember when my bus ride began or what time we arrived at the final stop.

"Last bus stop! Everybody come down!" the conductor shouted.

I stood up, clutching my bag tightly to my chest. Overwhelmed and bewildered, I simply followed the crowd and stepped off the bus. I had no idea where I was. My confusion must have been written all over my face.

"I hope you know where you are going?" an old lady asked.

"Er… er… where is this place, ma?" I stammered.

"This is Ojota. Where do you want to go?"

"Thank you, ma. Never mind, ma. I will be alright by myself."

"Okay," she said and walked away.

I was dazed by the sheer size of everything—massive bridges, countless vehicles, and an overwhelming number of people moving too fast for my mind to process. A crippling fear washed over me. I stood frozen in place.

An okada rider nearly hit me but sped past without stopping. Another missed me by a hair, then stopped to curse me, calling me a witch and hurling insults in a language I did not understand.

When I recovered, I spotted a cemented sidewalk with a raised platform, slightly removed from the chaos of okadas and other vehicles. I made my way there, under an overhead bridge, and sat down.

Tired, hungry, and thirsty, with no idea where to go, I lowered my head onto my small bag resting on my lap.

A loud voice roused me: "Pure water! Pure water!"

"How much is pure water?" I asked.

"N5.00 for one."

"Give me two," I said.

"That's ₦10," he replied.

I pulled out my last ₦10 note, handed it to him, and took two sachets of water. I drank both quickly.

I sat back, resting my head on my bag again. Thoughts of my life and my current situation filled my mind. I saw no hope, no comfort. Silent tears streamed down my face.

I wondered, if I cried loudly and drew attention, what would I say if people asked how I ended up here? I silently prayed for a quiet death.

I must have dozed off because I was suddenly yanked awake by a rough hand grabbing my neck.

"Bring that bag!" a voice shouted.

One of them snatched my bag and ran. The man holding me yanked my head backward, shining a torchlight in my face.

"She's a beautiful small gal. Let's take her and go play with her," he said to his accomplice.

The one who had taken my bag hesitated, then returned. They started dragging me down into a large gutter by the pavement.

I screamed.

"Keep quiet, or we'll kill you," they threatened.

But death was exactly what I wanted. So I screamed even louder.

A vehicle screeched to a halt nearby. The men abandoned me and fled, leaving my bag behind.

A tall, muscular man stepped out and walked toward me.

"What happened? Who were those people? What are you doing here at this time of night?" he asked.

I had no answers. I just kept crying.

When I still said nothing, he shone his phone's flashlight on my face, sizing me up. Satisfied that I wasn't a threat, he picked up my bag and took my hand, leading me to his vehicle.

He opened the back door and placed my bag inside before turning back to me.

"Come to the front so I can keep an eye on you," he said.

Perhaps he thought I might be dangerous and didn't want me sitting alone in the back where I could plot something.

He opened the back door again, took my hand, and guided me to the front seat.

As we drove, he kept asking questions.

"Who are you?"

I didn't answer. I just cried.

"Well, young lady, you have to tell me who you are. Otherwise, I'll take you to the police station."

When I still said nothing, he sighed and introduced himself instead.

"My name is Mr. Usang. I work in my own company in Victoria Island. The place you stopped today is a dangerous place in the evenings for even grown men, not to mention a little girl."

"So, what are you doing here?"

"Sir, I don't know. I am in trouble. I am running to nowhere that I know. Dying is the best for me now."

"Don't talk like that, young woman. We all face challenges in life. What matters is how you react to the problem. It is always important to hope that all will be well," he said.

"What is your name?"

"My name is Sarah, and I don't know why I am still alive."

"Hey! Young lady, stop talking like that. Where there is life, there is hope for good. And life is good, I assure you."

"My life has not been good at all. As we speak, I do not know where I am, and I cannot even say who I am."

"Okay, enough of that now. When we get to my home, you will get refreshed, and we can talk better."

"Ah! Sir, please don't take me to your home. Every home I have entered in the last two years, I have left with more trouble."

"Don't worry yourself, Sarah. You will be okay from now on."

I wished he was right.

After about an hour or so, wading through both heavy and light traffic, we arrived at his home.

A gateman opened the gate, and when we drove in, I noticed that he peeped into the vehicle and seemed to size me up under the floodlight.

Mr. Usang helped me out of the car and picked up my small bag from the back. As I stepped out, I surveyed the compound and saw wealth beyond anything I had ever encountered. It was a large compound with well-landscaped flower beds and trees. As far as the floodlights allowed me to see, there was only one building in the entire expansive, beautiful compound.

When he pressed the car horn, I expected children or maybe a wife to come out to welcome us. Instead, only one man emerged. He did not look like a relative of Mr. Usang at all.

"Good evening, sir. Welcome, sir," the man said.

"Aha! Effiong, get my bag and some items from the trunk," Mr. Usang instructed.

"Sarah, come with me," he added.

If Mr. Usang's compound was breathtaking, his living room was out of this world. I had never seen anything like it before. As soon as I stepped inside, I froze, afraid to put my filthy feet on the beautiful Arabian rug or the chrome-rimmed sofas. The flowers, the aquarium filled with goldfish (I only learned it was an aquarium after two days in the house)—everything felt surreal.

Mr. Usang encouraged me to keep moving and motioned toward a sofa near the large-screen TV on the wall. The air conditioning in the room was an experience I had never felt before in my life.

I had thought that Mr. Adeleke was the richest man in the world, but Mr. Usang's house made Mr. Adeleke's home look like Nurse Eliza's village if one were to compare them.

Effiong entered, laden with some provisions and Mr. Usang's briefcase.

"Effiong, when you drop what you are carrying, go and fix the visitor's room for our guest. Clean it up, freshen it with air freshener, and make sure you provide soap, toothpaste and a toothbrush, body lotion, and toiletries," Mr. Usang directed.

"Yes, ugah," Effiong responded.

I sat at the edge of the seat, wondering what on earth I was doing in a fairyland like this.

When Effiong reported that he had prepared the room, Mr. Usang thanked him and asked me to follow him. He led me upstairs on a fully carpeted staircase, the red rug soft beneath my feet. He showed me into the room and told me to feel at home.

"Sarah, take your bath and change your clothes. Keep the ones you are wearing—Effiong will wash them for you tomorrow. As soon as food is ready, I will call you."

When he left, I undressed, wrapped a towel around my body, and went into the bathroom. However, I could not figure out how to get the water to flow. The bathroom had a bathtub, unlike the one in my aunt's house.

At my aunt's place, our bathroom had a shower and a plain floor. I usually fetched water in a bucket to bathe so I wouldn't get my hair wet. In Nurse Eliza's house, it was an open bathroom where we carried water in a bucket from the tap in the compound to a makeshift bathing area.

I fumbled with the fixtures until, suddenly, water began splashing everywhere in the room, and I panicked. I screamed for help.

Mr. Usang ran to my door, knocking and asking what was wrong. As I kept shouting, he opened the door and saw me struggling to control the showerhead, which was spraying water all over me and the floor.

"Sarah! Are you alright? Should I come in and help?"

"Yes, sir!"

He entered the bathroom. I felt a little shy, barely covered. As soon as he stepped in, he seemed momentarily frozen, his gaze lingering on my body. That made me self-conscious, and I unknowingly dropped the shower nozzle, causing water to splash onto Mr. Usang's face and body.

He let out a startled laugh, jumping back, which made me laugh as well. It was funny.

For a moment, we locked eyes. I felt a sudden, unexpected wave of desire. Quickly, I pulled myself together and turned away.

He cleared his throat, heaved a sigh of relief, and only said, "Wow!" Then he turned off the water.

"Were you having problems with the shower?" he asked.

"Yes," I responded.

"Here is how it is done."

He proceeded to show me how to adjust the water, explaining how I could set it for hot or cold, depending on my preference. He also told me I could fill the bathtub, soak inside, and drain the water afterward.

He had probably taken his own bath earlier. Now in pajamas, he smelled very fine when he came close to me. Under the bright fluorescent light in the bathroom, I could see that he was a very tall, handsome man, with tinges of gray around the edges of his hair.

When he left, I filled the bathtub with warm water, lowered myself inside, and felt as though I could stay there forever. It was so soothing, both to my wearied body and my troubled mind.

When I finished, I changed into my newest evening dress and came down to the sitting room. He was already waiting, now dressed in another set of pajamas.

"Ah! There you are, Sarah. I have been waiting for you so we could eat."

I was speechless. *Wait for me? Why?* I kept asking myself.

Shyly, I joined him at the huge dining table, sitting at the other end, opposite him. I was clearly intimidated by the table setting and hesitated, unsure of how to begin. He probably noticed and came over to help. He scooped food onto the plate in front of me and handed me a spoon, fork, and knife.

I dropped the fork and knife and started eating with the spoon. When I looked at him, he was eating with the knife and fork. I watched him for a while. He raised his head and noticed. Our eyes met again, and he smiled.

"Is there anything I should help you with?" he asked.

"No, sir. I was just watching how you eat with a fork and knife, like people I see on TV," I responded.

"Ahh! Hmmmm!" he said and smiled.

I was treated to the best meal I had ever had—rice, plantain, chicken, vegetables, and stew, with a cup of fruit juice. I had never eaten anything like it in my entire life.

When we finished, Effiong came and cleared the table. Mr. Usang gestured for me to take a seat in the living room.

"As soon as the food settles, I would like to hear your story. I want to know what a pretty little girl like you was doing in that evil place at night," Mr. Usang said.

"Sir, where is your family? Your wife and children?" I ventured to ask.

"They are on holiday in London," he said.

"Where is London?" I asked naively.

"It's overseas—the capital of England."

Without really knowing where that was, I simply said, "Oh, okay." I said nothing more, feeling too ignorant to continue the discussion.

"Sarah, would you mind telling me more about yourself and what made you go and hang out under that bridge—a known den of robbers?" Mr. Usang asked.

"Sir, I don't think you want to hear my story," I said hesitantly.

"Why not? I asked because I *do* want to hear it," he insisted.

"Hmmmmmm…"

Before I could start, tears filled my eyes. And before I could say a word, I was crying openly, choking on my sobs.

He came over, put his arms around me, and started consoling me. He wiped my tears, stroked my hair, and continued until I felt so comforted that I snuggled closer, resting my head on his chest.

There were no amorous thoughts in my mind at this time. This felt like being in the secure and safe hands of the father I had lost and longed for all these years. I fell asleep in his arms.

It must have been very peaceful because, when I woke up, he was still seated there, holding me as I lay tucked against his chest.

I felt torn—part of me wanted to stay there forever, to hold onto him tightly so I wouldn't lose this moment of comfort, but then I was suddenly alarmed as a thought of sex crossed my mind.

I pulled away abruptly.

"I'm sorry, sir. Have I caused you any trouble?" I managed to ask.

"No, Sarah, it's okay. I understand your situation. I have a daughter about your age," he said gently.

I moved to sit on another sofa nearby.

"Sir, I know I am supposed to tell you about myself and my situation. But it's difficult for me. I will try my best," I said hesitantly. "It's a long story, and I blame myself for my misfortunes."

"You're just a baby, judging by your age," he said. "Don't blame yourself for everything. It's all part of growing up."

I gave him a summary of my life as best as I could, explaining that my downward spiral had begun when the woman who helped deliver my child sold him—and then wanted me to stay with her to make more babies for her to sell.

"I was so disgusted that she saw me as nothing more than that. I couldn't stay there. So, I left—not really knowing what I was doing, partly hoping I would somehow die in the process, just to end the torture that my life has become. Thank you, Mr. Usang. As soon as it's daybreak, I'll continue my journey and hope it ends soon," I concluded.

"Don't talk like that, young lady. You've been through a lot, and that's a pity, but there are worse cases than yours. I can help you get back on your feet, build a life, and possibly even find your parents and brother. They are probably out there looking for you right now," he said.

"I doubt that, sir. Nothing has ever worked out for me before. I don't see why it would now," I said.

"Give yourself a break, young lady. You are too hard on yourself. Please stop, Sarah," he counseled.

"Okay, sir. Thank you for your encouragement," I said softly.

I stood up to go back to my room. As I walked a few steps away, I felt his gaze on me. I turned back and saw that he was watching me, admiration and intensity in his eyes. I blushed.

"Sarah, come back here, please. I'm worried about you being all alone. Come and sit here with me till daybreak, so I can be sure you'll be okay."

He was right in his assessment. I was worried to high heavens about what to do with myself. Yet, I felt at peace with him.

I went back. When I got close to him, he stretched out his arms, and I unabashedly fell into them. He held me so warmly and so close that my prematurely overgrown sensual nature was aroused. He must have felt the same way because, as he stroked my hair, I noticed his manhood awakening between his legs.

We clung to each other tighter and tighter. He tilted my head and kissed me on the forehead. Shivers ran all over my body. Then he kissed me deeply on the mouth, and I lost all resistance. The fire ignited between us was too much for either of us to control. He got up, with me still clinging to him, and carried me upstairs to my room.

We tore at each other ravenously, expressing the deep hunger for sexual intimacy that both of us had clearly been missing for a long time.

When I woke up the next morning and saw that we had slept in each other's arms, guilt and foolishness washed over me. I knew this cycle had never brought me any good.

What if I get pregnant again? I worried. *What if his wife and children return and find out? Where would I go next?*

Tears welled up, and I started sobbing. It must have been my loud crying that woke him. His face looked so satisfied and at peace, but that changed when he saw my tears.

"What is it, Sarah? Come, my sweet baby, come," he entreated.

"No, sir," I protested. "It's this same act that brought me all my woes. I don't know how I keep getting into this," I lamented.

"Oh, Sarah, I've told you not to be so hard on yourself. What happened today was sweet. You saw how hungry we both were for intimacy. It is love," Mr. Usang said.

"It cannot be love, sir. How can love cause so much pain? I feel like, having been accustomed to sex, we were both simply starved. Your wife has been away for three weeks, and for over two years, I haven't had any sexual intercourse—when before, I was having a double dose. This cannot be love, sir," I argued.

"Ah! Sarah, I don't know what to say. I felt love between us," he said.

"Well, sir, my problem now is that the last time I got involved in sex—my rapes and then my subsequent consensual intercourse with Mr. Adeleke and his son, Gbenga—I ended up pregnant. I lost my family. I became a vagabond. I endured the trauma and torture of carrying a pregnancy, giving birth, and having my son sold by Nurse Eliza. My life was at risk, and you rescued me.

If I start again with you, and then your wife comes back, I'll be out on the streets again. And you might lose your family. Now I'm terrified of what will happen now that we've done this."

"Well, Sarah, that thought had crossed my mind ever since I started feeling this way about you. I told myself I was supposed to protect you. When I heard your story, my desire to be your protector grew even stronger. But this feeling of love kept coming in between.

Now we've done it, and it was sweet and comforting. We can't stop now. Don't worry, young lady—I'll take care of you. I'll take care of the situation," he assured me.

"Sir, Mr. Adeleke told me the same thing. And what did I get? Pregnancy, abandonment, misery, and a life on the streets. You cannot be different. You have a family. They will be hurt and angry.

I may be a child, but I now know how these things happen. As soon as your wife returns, you won't be able to explain my presence here, and I'll be on the street again. Sir, I suggest we treat last night as pure madness—a terrible mistake we must never repeat.

As you go to work this morning, I need to be on my way again."

"No, Sarah! You could be my daughter. I won't allow you to be on the street again. We'll find a way. I love you," he confessed.

"Sir, it is not love. It is sex. I may not fully understand love, but I know what we did. We had simple, animalistic sex. We both desired it, so we did it. That does not make it love."

"Okay, Sarah, soothe yourself," he said. "But I am not letting you out on the street for any reason."

That morning, before leaving for work, he gave me money and asked Effiong to accompany me to a nearby clothing shop to get some clean clothes.

Later, after finishing his morning chores, Effiong approached me.

"Small madam, you go share with me ooo," he said, flashing a big smile.

At first, I felt angry that he called me "small madam." But then I saw the smile on his face and thought that maybe he wasn't being derisive. So, I decided to be conversational.

"Hmmmmm! Effiong, what am I sharing with you?"

"Ah, small madam, me I dey share *efryting* ooo. If *ugah* give you money, you must give me my cut. And I dey do the other one too," he said, laughing, his eyes holding that familiar, disgusting look—the one men give when they see women as nothing more than sex objects.

Now, I felt he was being derisive.

"Hush! Effiong, I cannot allow you to insult me. Stop right there or…"

"Or what, small madam?" he asked sagaciously. "No play with me ooo. The last woman wey try am, ugah madam come back suddenly, come meet am here, and pour am acid. No play with me ooo. Only those who share efryting with me na dem dey stay enjoy my ugah well well."

I was alarmed to learn of this blackmail situation, which meant that I would have to share money with Effiong and also have sex with him. I made efforts to subdue my growing annoyance. Fearing I would end up in another Adeleke Gbenga situation, I decided to inform Mr. Usang when he arrived home from work.

"Em em, ugah Ee…ffiong! I hear you. No skin pain. Let's go this market and come back, you hear?" I managed to lie.

Feeling assured now—or trying to deepen his veiled threats—he proceeded to recount how he dealt with some of the women who saw him as nothing and refused to share.

"My ugah no no say, ugah madam buy phone give me and tell me to hide am well well. She buy me plenty credit and give me money and say anytime any woman come house come sleep with ugah, make me I flash am so that she go come quick quick come deal with that woman.

"But I like my ugah well well. Him dey extend hand correct. So, when any woman don come, I go give my ugah some space to enjoy. I dey strike after the first or second visit, depending on how things dey torchlight. Then, I go ask the woman to share, and if she refuses, I call ugah madam, and she go come cause problem, and that one go run. The last one, my madam pour acid give am."

"Ok, Effiong bobo, no worries. Make we return market and see how things go waka, you hear."

"Alright, small madam. Efrything about you is good," Effiong concluded.

We did not have any other conversations except when he directed me where to get some of the things we were looking for.

History was now making me angry, and I had to stop him before I lost my cool and let him know that I would be informing Mr. Usang.

In the intervening days and weeks, Effiong continued to be nice to me. He would take care of my every need. He even suggested different ways I could enjoy myself while staying at Mr. Usang's home. I could feel his increasing awkwardness around me, yet he made sure I lacked nothing.

I put in every effort I could muster to wish away Effiong's blackmail, but the foreboding of an explosion would not go away. I continued to feel that his being nice to me was like feeding a Christmas chicken—so much effort was expended to help the chicken grow bigger and fatter, only to have it slaughtered on Christmas Eve or Christmas Day.

For one thing, I was sure I would not enter the vicious cycle of having sex with both Mr. Usang and Effiong. Apart from the obvious social situation between the two of them, I could not forget in a hurry my experience with Mr. Adeleke and his son Gbenga.

Some three weeks into my stay in Mr. Usang's house, Effiong came to get his share.

"Small madam, you fine well well. Efrything about you, fine," Effiong said one morning after Mr. Usang had gone to work.

He moved to touch me as he spoke, but I dodged, held my head with my hands, and feigned tiredness and a headache. I informed Effiong that I needed to sleep to ensure that he would not come and bother me.

That night, when Mr. Usang sneaked into my room, I expected him to ask for more sex, but I told him I needed to leave his house before the calamity that followed me everywhere I went came to his family.

He hushed me and produced a pack of gifts he had bought for me. I refused his gifts and asked him to leave so that we would not become too attached, making it too painful when I eventually left.

He countered that I was not going to leave his house unless I was able to take care of myself. He added that he had a plan to help me get a good life—learn a trade, start a business, or go to school.

I wondered and asked him if his wife was not returning and where we would be staying to make all his tall plans for me work out.

"That would not work, sir," I told him.

"Why not? I am the one doing it, and you say it would not work?"

"Sir, Effiong has asked me to share the money you give me and have sex with him. Otherwise, he would call madam and tell her that you have a woman in the house. He said that he has been doing that with all the women who came to the house."

"What?" he shouted. "But that is not possible. My wife went to London. Effiong does not have a phone. So how would he tell my wife? Before my wife comes back, I would have found a house for you and settled you there."

"Effiong said that your wife bought him a secret phone, which he has hidden. He said he was the one that informed your wife about some women, making her return suddenly to drive them out of the house with acid," I informed Mr. Usang.

"I will kill that scoundrel. Oh, so it is him. I have been accusing my wife of witchcraft and really been afraid of how she used to know. He will leave this house tomorrow morning," Mr. Usang threatened.

This revelation must have killed the sexual urge in him. He kept asking me not to worry, assuring me that he would take care of everything soon.

The next morning, he called Effiong to bring his phone. I overheard Effiong swear that he had no phone. Mr. Usang dragged him by the neck to his room and held him until he brought out the phone. Then, he asked him to pack his belongings and leave the house immediately. That early morning, he threw Effiong out of the house.

Before he left for work, Mr. Usang asked me if I could cook and keep the house. I said I could, though I might not be able to cook as well as Effiong.

He said, "Anyhow you can cook, do it. Keep the house clean, and anything you can cook, we will eat it like that."

I worked hard all day and was able to clean up the house. Nurse Eliza had taught me how to cook, so I was able to make food. When Mr. Usang came back, he ate and claimed to have enjoyed it. He thanked me with a hug and a kiss on the forehead. That night, we slept in his bedroom and had sex. It was a cozy experience.

The nagging feeling of looming danger did not stop. I continued to be afraid that I was going to be in deep trouble. The fear was so strong that I even had a bad dream where I was beaten to death by Mr. Usang's wife and some thugs she had hired.

After about a week of peace, the day I had feared so much finally came.

I was alone in the house. Mr. Usang had, as usual, gone to Victoria Island for work. I felt lonesome and decided to chat with the gateman. After a few minutes of chatting, I felt quite bored and decided to stroll to a nearby shop to look around and possibly buy something to lift my spirits.

I spent quite some time out there. When I strolled back to Mr. Usang's house, I saw the gate man outside. He was always inside the compound for as long as I had known him. As soon as I approached, he took a few steps toward me and announced in hushed tones that Big Madam had come back.

"She eye dey red like hot pepper. Say if she eye catch you, she eye go kill you dead with her hand. Please, no go into that compound." That is why I am outside—to stop you from going in," the poor, alarmed gate man counseled.

"Baba, thank you," I managed to say in horror.

"Effiong follow Madam come. Na him tell Oga Madam say you dey house. Na so Effiong dey do all the time. Him say after Oga drive am comot for house, he carry Madam number wey him write for book, dey call Oga Madam, so tey Oga Madam come pick him call. Na so Oga Madam take know," the gate man added.

Tears started running down my cheeks. I could not voice my crying. My worst fears had come true so quickly again.

I cried, "Oh God, since I cannot find any way to live on my own terms, please take my life. I am tired. If only I knew how to live without having these men in my life. If only I was a boy and of no sexual value to these men, maybe my life would be different. Maybe not. Maybe I would have been able to die without the intervention of these men. If only I knew how to die by myself. Whatever, oh God, take my life and let me be."

I kept lamenting as I continued walking ahead, without knowing where I was going.

Of all my worldly possessions, I had just a half-jean trouser and a small blouse on me. I did not even put on a bra when I went out that day and moved around for days without one—for God knows how long—before Mrs. Akinyemi picked me up from the edge of a deep drainage filled with dirty water that I wanted to jump into some years ago.

Since I left Mr. Usang's house, all I had done was wander from place to place, sleeping in abandoned sheds, open mechanic workshops, and wherever night and sleep found me—for only God knows how long—begging for food along the way.

A few times, I tried to work at building sites, but either the rough boys wanted to rape me, or they stole the little money I was paid. So, for a period I could not reckon, I wandered about, doing whatever I could to get food or find a place to sleep.

Initially, I worked in a bukateria, but when they discovered that I had nowhere to sleep or bathe daily, they could not cope with a girl who did not take her bath.

On that fateful day, I had been jolted from sleep by a thunderstorm and heavy rain, with a whirlwind that blew off the roof of the open, empty motorcycle mechanic shed I had entered when the rain started drizzling that night.

I had walked all day to nowhere and was worn out, tired, and hungry. I must have fallen asleep as soon as I entered that shed.

I was in the middle of a terrifying dream. I saw my father being flogged by prison officials, and he was crying. I was crying too, running toward him, and in the distance, I saw my brother James also crying and running away—to nowhere in particular.

When the whirlwind tore through the thatch covering the shed, the rain poured on me and woke me up. I was crying from the dream into real life.

As I woke up, I saw that the day had broken. Many people were running helter-skelter from the rain, which was now heavier and thundering that morning. Several vehicles, including those yellow buses I had seen a few weeks ago when I first arrived in these parts, were everywhere.

In my despair, I turned around, not really knowing where I should go next. I noticed a huge drainage system with a big surge of water flowing inside it, making a loud noise. The furious current carried along chunks of debris—broken wooden chairs, plastic objects, and other household waste—smashing them against the drainage walls as the water flowed. From time to time, a huge chunk of green algae would float along with the surging water.

For some time, I just fixed my eyes on the rushing water until the idea came into my mind: if I jumped into the drainage, I could easily drown, and that would settle everything once and for all.

The first time I gave in to the thought, a chilling feeling came over me, and I trembled. I instinctively took a few steps backward. But then, the troubles I had been through—homeless again and again in my short life—filled my heart and made it heavy. I decided I had to end this life so my pain could go away. The dream about my father and James filled my mind.

My heart started pounding heavily. I moved from sobbing to real crying. Each time I thought of making the jump to end it all, palpable fear seized my whole body. I would shudder and step back.

I had just let out a loud yell and made a run to jump into the drainage—full to the brim with rushing, dirty water—when a woman yelled after me.

"Young girl! Stop right there! What do you think you are doing?"

I turned around and saw an elderly woman running after me, pointing at me and shouting, "Stop there! Stop there! Right now! What do you think you are doing? Are you out of your mind? You want to kill yourself?"

She kept shouting at me until she reached me, where I now stood, stupefied and crying.

She grabbed my hand and dragged me away from the drainage to her house, which was almost directly opposite the location of the huge drainage.

She held my hand tightly and pulled me inside. Once inside her clean but simple room, she made me sit on a wooden bench, then sat beside me and asked, "What were you thinking, trying to jump into that drainage? That would have killed you instantly!"

"That's exactly what I wanted, Ma. I want to die. I cannot continue. Life has been bad for me for as long as I can remember. So, dying is the best and only thing left. At least if I die—"

"Hush now, dear young girl!"

She turned me around and looked me in the face.

"This voice—I recognize it. Are you not the same girl I watched on the bus about a month or two ago? You asked me where we were, and I told you it was Ojota?"

I looked at her intently and realized she was the woman I had spoken to when I first arrived.

"Yes, it is me, Ma."

"Oh, heavens!" she exclaimed. "Your voice of anguish has never left my mind. I have suffered the regret of allowing you to leave my presence that day. Something kept telling me I should have pushed my fears aside and tried to find out what was disturbing you.

"Oh my God, I am so sorry I did not act upon the prompting of the Spirit to ask after your condition and why you looked so agitated and confused that day."

"What happened to you? Where is the bag you were carrying that day?" she asked all at once.

"It is a long story, Ma. I don't think you want to hear it."

"What nonsense is that? Why wouldn't I want to hear it, when I am the one asking?" she queried.

"Er... er... er...!"

A heavy surge of tears and choking overtook me, and I broke down, crying loudly.

"Okay, okay, okay," she said. "Stop now. Don't worry. Just stop crying."

She rubbed my back to soothe me.

"Give me a moment. I'll be back," she said and left me, disappearing into her bedroom.

She emerged shortly with a glass of refreshingly cool water.

"Here, young girl, drink this," she said.

I grabbed the water with both hands and drank it all up, bowing as I took the cup. It had been some time since I had good, cool, clean water to drink, and this seemed to have a real calming effect on my body.

"What is your name?"

"My name is Sarah, ma."

"Okay, Sarah, I have put water on the fire for you. When it is boiled, you can take your bath, and I will see how I can help you."

I took my bath, and Mrs. Akinyemi gave me a fresh oversized blouse and a gown of hers to wear. I felt really refreshed. As soon as I finished changing into the dress she gave me, she invited me to have a meal. It was well-made rice and stew with fried plantain.

When I finished eating, I took the dishes into the kitchen and started washing them. Mrs. Akinyemi came in, looked at me, and nodded her head in approval of my manners. Later, she commended me, saying that children nowadays no longer remember proper manners, and she was happy that I had not forgotten what my mother taught me. Her words made me both happy and sad as I remembered my mother.

Sensing my emotions, she reassured me, asking me to let her know when I was ready to talk about what had happened and why I had been on the street all this time. I was relieved to have someone willing to listen. My initial attempts to speak were filled with tears, and she continued to comfort me kindly.

"My daughter, whatever it is, it will pass. Very soon, you will not remember the pain anymore," she said gently.

Though her words brought some comfort, I couldn't shake the feeling that my troubles were far from over.

When I finally mustered the courage to speak, I told her as briefly as I could about the calamity that had befallen me—from the day of my rape to the present. She cried openly with me when my own tears wouldn't stop. Drawing close, she held me and encouraged me to plan for a new life from that moment forward.

"All will be well in the end," she assured me. "God watches over His children, even in their afflictions."

Though my life experiences made that hard to believe, she left me hoping that maybe, just maybe, things would truly get better.

She then shared some of her own struggles as a young woman. Though she had never been raped or thrown out, she had lost her parents at an early age and was raised by different relatives and sometimes even neighbors. She faced much tribulation and suffering, but what helped her was a decision she made in secondary school—to become a notable person, like some of her great schoolteachers and the inspiring characters she read about in books.

When night came, Mrs. Akinyemi showed me to my room.

"This is your room," she said warmly. "Make it your home for as long as you want or need."

She lived alone in a three-bedroom apartment on the ground floor of a block of flats. She told me that she and her husband had purchased the flat many years ago. Since their retirement, they had lived there together until her husband passed away a year and a half ago.

The Akinyemis had three grown children, all married and living abroad. Mrs. Akinyemi was usually alone, except for occasional visits from her children and grandchildren. One of her nephews visited from time to time and was expected back in a few weeks.

She was an elderly woman aging gracefully. She did not seem excessively wealthy, but she appeared to have enough to live comfortably. She carried herself with confidence, showing no fear about anything. I wished I could have such a life.

Her kitchen was large—about the same size as Mr. Usang's kitchen. She seemed to love it, as it was beautifully furnished with modern cooking equipment and utensils. Cabinets lined both the walls and the floor, and a large refrigerator and deep freezer made her seem well-off at her level.

The next morning, she woke up early—around 5:30 a.m. When I heard her moving around in the kitchen, which was close to my room, I came out and greeted her. She was so happy that she stopped, called me her daughter, and wished me good morning.

"The frenzy of yesterday didn't allow us to discuss my routine," she said. "I wake up at 5:30 a.m. every morning. I drink some water, say a prayer, and study the scriptures—if there's light, either from the public supply or my rechargeable lamps. Then I prepare for the day and leave the house at 7 a.m. for my shop at the Ojota Shopping Plaza."

"What do you sell in your shop, Mummy?" I asked.

"I deal in fashion and jewelry," she said joyfully. "I make my own fashion designs and sell matching jewelry—both beads and precious metals. We also make beads in my shop."

"Wow! I wish I could make dresses like you, Mummy."

"Oh, if you're interested, you can learn."

"I am interested! When can I begin?"

"You can come to the shop tomorrow and start. Two new trainees are beginning tomorrow. You can be the third."

I was enthralled by the prospect of having a meaningful life. I had always loved fashion, starting from childhood when I enjoyed the secondhand clothing my mother brought home from the market where she and my father worked. I admired people who dressed well and always wished I could do the same.

I was beside myself with happiness—I almost burst with joy.

And so, a new life began for me.

For the next four months, Mrs. Akinyemi and I left home together every day for the fashion workshop. She encouraged me to pay attention to the training and practice, so I could gain the skill quickly and help her in the shop. She proposed that once I learned how to make dresses, I should also learn the business side of things, so I could one day set up my own shop.

Life with Mrs. Akinyemi seemed almost too good to be true. Before long, I started feeling that things were moving too fast—too perfectly. It felt surreal. I tried to silence the doubts creeping into my mind, wondering if I even deserved such kindness.

But through it all, she never once referred to my painful past or treated me as anything less than her own child.

The days, weeks, and months passed so quickly that I stopped keeping track. I was so enthralled with my new life that I did not see it coming.

It was a school vacation when one of Mrs. Akinyemi's young nephews came to spend the holiday with her. He came from Ijebu-Ode. Babajide Odumosu, an 18-year-old boy, was handsome but had a perpetually sad expression. He was the son of Mrs. Akinyemi's younger brother, a man who had never done well for himself and constantly relied on her generosity. Jide, as he was popularly called, had lived with his often-drunken father all his life. He was reportedly too much for his parents to handle, so arrangements were made for him to spend the long vacation with Mrs. Akinyemi, in the hope that he might find discipline and improve his behavior.

His arrival filled me with a sense of foreboding, reinforcing the unease I had been feeling for weeks. Since he arrived, we had merely greeted each other courteously. There had been no direct contact or confrontation, yet I couldn't shake the feeling that a clash was inevitable. His presence made me taciturn, fidgety, and irritable. I even started making mistakes both at home and at the shop, to the point that one of my trainers pulled me aside, asking if something was wrong and offering to help if needed.

Mrs. Akinyemi also noticed that I was not as coordinated as I used to be. One day, in passing, she asked if I was alright. Not wanting her to probe further—especially since I had no real answers—I quickly responded that I was okay and just had a slight headache. She advised me to drink some water and said that if the headache persisted until the next day, she would take me to the hospital for a checkup in case I had malaria or some other illness.

Her concern reminded me of my auntie back home, who would always dismiss my fatigue and headaches in a similar manner. That realization made me even more anxious. After all, Mr. Usang and I had been having sex regularly just months ago. However, I pushed that fear aside, knowing that my real source of distress was the presence of this sad-faced boy—Babajide Odumosu.

By the time Jide had spent a week with us, he felt confident enough to engage me in conversation. Until then, we had continued minding our own business, exchanging only the most basic greetings—"Good morning," "Good afternoon," "Good evening"— without any real interest or sense of familial responsibility.

Our first conversation was awkward. I felt no affinity for him and had no idea what we could possibly discuss. Until that day, the only words we had exchanged were the "welcome" I offered when Mrs. Akinyemi introduced him and our occasional formal greetings. There was a clear and mutual distance between us.

His first words to me in this conversation were childish and uncultured.

"Hey! Girl, what did you say your name is again?"

"I never told you my name," I responded.

My reply seemed to catch him off guard. A look of discomfort crossed his face, and he quickly stepped aside, ending the conversation before it could begin. His withdrawal relieved the awkwardness of our interaction, at least for the moment.

Several more days passed before Jide attempted to speak with me again. This time, it happened after Mrs. Akinyemi expressed concern that the two of us were not getting along. Seizing the moment, he said, "Aunty mi, ask her for me. I don't understand her at all."

Mrs. Akinyemi didn't dwell on it. She simply moved on with her business, probably thinking she had created the perfect opportunity for us to connect.

Hearing the arrogance in Jide's voice, I didn't bother responding to his accusatory remark. I simply walked away, just as Mrs. Akinyemi had.

Another opportunity for interaction arose when she assigned both of us the task of cleaning out the storage room, which was filled with household items, both old and new. The room had been left untouched for a long time, and many of the items were covered in dust or already spoiling.

Jide was careless with the work, dragging his feet and wasting time on each item. At one point, he dragged a small table across the floor instead of picking it up, creating an awful noise. I called out to him, telling him to lift the table rather than dragging it.

He stopped, gave me a derisive look, and then suddenly screamed, "Ahhhh! See what you've done now."

"Jide, what is it? Why are you talking to me like that?" I asked.

"Blind girl, can't you see that you distracted me with your talking? Now I've dragged the table over my big toe. Look—blood everywhere!"

"Oh yeah? Dumb ass. You can't even take care of yourself," I shot back.

That infuriated him. He completely lost his temper, throwing the corn cob he had been eating at me, intending to hurt me. I barely dodged in time.

He muttered curses in his native language, words I couldn't understand. Yet, I felt a strange mix of excitement and fear—excited that this sad-faced boy couldn't control me, but also afraid that if I wasn't careful, he might actually hurt me. For the rest of the week, I made a conscious effort to avoid him.

Jide and I continued this cat-and-dog relationship for several weeks.

The night before *that* day—the fateful day that still sends shudders through me—I had terrible nightmares. I woke up multiple times, sweating and trembling, chased in my dreams by people wielding machetes and clubs. In one dream, I was running from something I can't even remember, only to be knocked down by a vehicle. In another, I slipped into a deep gully and was carried away by a dirty, over-flooded drainage system. Each time, I woke up with a scream, my heart pounding.

That morning, I was so shaken that even Mrs. Akinyemi noticed.

"What's wrong?" she asked.

"I had terrible nightmares last night. Not one, not two, but more than three times."

"What happened in your dreams?" she asked.

I recounted them all. The worried look on her face made me even more afraid.

She told me to kneel for prayers. In that moment, I experienced the most intimate mother-daughter connection I had ever felt. She poured out her heart, asking God to protect me and preserve my life. Then she blessed me:

"God will protect you!"

"Amen!"

"Your enemies will not get you!"

"Amen!"

"No weapon fashioned against you will prosper!"

"Amen!"

"It is your enemies that will drown!"

"Amen!"

"In the name of Jesus Christ, Amen!"

"Aaami!"

When we rose from the prayer, I felt some peace. However, that peace was short-lived as Mrs. Akinyemi announced then and there that she would be traveling to Ijebu-Ode the next day to attend a family meeting in preparation for the burial rites of a deceased family member. A very important matriarch of the Odumosu family had died some months ago, and the family, both at home and abroad, was meeting that weekend to plan for the burial.

She counseled me to take care of the house and ensure that I went to the shop every day to learn the trade and keep an eye on things.

"Sarah, you will be my eyes and ears in the shop. See to it that nothing goes wrong. If you notice anything, take careful note, and if you can prevent trouble, please be bold enough to speak up so the people involved will see that you know what is going on," she said.

For the entire day, the foreboding of staying alone in the house with that brutish Jide overshadowed my whole being. I became listless and made a lot more mistakes. I could see that Mrs. Akinyemi herself was quite unsettled.

"Sarah, are you sure you're alright? Is there anything you want to tell me that's making you uncomfortable? Do you need an explanation for anything? I feel you're already conversant with what we do here and can keep a tidy house, so I'm confident you'll be able to take care of things and be perfectly fine," she added.

While escorting her to the car that morning with her traveling bag, tears filled my eyes. I tried unsuccessfully to stifle them, but they flowed uncontrollably. I barely managed to suppress the urge to cry out loud. I felt devastated by the thought of being left alone in the house with that awful Jide.

My mood, fears, and thoughts did not seem to be entirely lost on Mrs. Akinyemi. As we stood beside her vehicle, she began admonishing me to be strong, careful, and wise while she was away, assuring me that she wouldn't be gone for too long.

"I'll be returning in two days," she said.

I just nodded, unable to utter a word. Any attempt would have led to loud sobbing.

I opened her car door and helped her inside, adjusting her wrappers so they wouldn't get caught in the door. As I closed it and waved her goodbye, I felt as though I had been locked out of existence. I couldn't understand the feeling. Mrs. Akinyemi had been my entire life for the past year, and her leaving, even for a few days, felt like being shut out of life itself for eternity.

Almost unconsciously, I walked to the gate and opened it. As the driver pulled out in Mrs. Akinyemi's old-model Chevrolet, I had the overwhelming urge to run after her and never return to the house that had been my home—my heaven on earth—this past year.

If I had acted on that impulse that day, I might never have been caught in the trouble that eventually forced me to hurriedly and painfully escape from Mrs. Akinyemi's home, burdened with a weight on my soul to this day.

When I locked the gate and returned to the house, I seriously considered just leaving and never coming back. However, with no idea where I would go, I sat down on my bed, confused, worried, and lost in thought. Tears streamed down my face, falling onto my lap. I felt hopeless, helpless, alone, and afraid, overwhelmed by a heavy sense of impending doom.

I don't remember how long I remained in that state. It felt as though I had drifted into a daze, a half-conscious reverie, when I suddenly heard a coarse voice and felt two rough hands shaking me by the shoulders.

I jolted awake, shocked and terrified to see Jide standing over me, gripping my shoulders tightly and shouting my name.

When I came to, I yelled at him and shoved him with all the strength I could muster, pushing him away from me.

"Get out of my room, idiot! How dare you come in here without knocking and without being invited?"

Before he could respond, I screamed again. "Get out… get out… get out!!!"

He resisted my shoving and yelled back at me. "Nonsense! Nonsense!! Nonsense, girl!!! You can't push me out of my own house. This entire house belongs to me! You are my servant. My aunty has traveled, so I'm in charge now. Stop your nonsense and come serve me food."

"Oh yeah? Me? Your servant? You're going to starve to death before 'your aunty' returns if you can't take care of yourself. Now leave my room if you know what's good for you!" I shouted back.

He stormed out, cursing and muttering in his native language— words I couldn't understand. The only thing I caught as he went outside was, "This girl sef, you no know me ooo!"

For the rest of the day, I tried to push Jide out of my mind, but it was useless. The fear of what he might do to me at night crept in. I was restless in my soul and sluggish in my movements. All kinds of terrifying thoughts swirled in my head.

Before long, images flashed in my mind—visions of him raping me, beating me, unimaginable horrors. It was as if I were paralyzed. I couldn't move. I didn't go to the shop. I just sat on my bed, worrying, crying, sobbing. It was a nightmare in broad daylight.

I didn't eat. I was completely beside myself with fear and dread.

The next thing I realized, it was evening. This awareness came when Jide walked into my room again, looking fierce, sweating, and reeking of cigarette smoke and what smelled like Indian hemp.

He was practically barking.

"This foolish gal, where is my foooood?" he drawled, chewing gum as he spoke.

I was so terrified that I could barely find my voice. The fears that had plagued me all day flooded back with full force.

I managed to mutter, "Jide, as you can see, I'm not feeling well. There's food in the kitchen. Please go fix yourself something and leave me alone."

Jide responded to my simple request with a stunning slap that sent me reeling to the floor. Before I could gasp, he was on me, beating the hell out of me, cursing in his native tongue.

Then he grabbed my throat with his left hand and, with his right, began tearing off my skirt and underwear while squeezing the life out of me.

I was losing breath when, suddenly, I remembered a story Nurse Eliza once told me—how she had escaped being raped by her aunt's husband when she was just seventeen.

This "uncle" had tried every trick in the book to lure her into sex with him, without success. On that fateful weekend morning, they were alone in the house as her aunt had gone to an early morning market to buy food. She was in the kitchen working on her chores when the man came in, grabbed her from behind, and pinned her to the ground.

As he knelt over her and pulled down his pajamas, she grabbed his scrotum, squeezed, and pulled as hard as she could. The man screamed at the top of his voice, jumped off her body, and fell flat to the ground—giving her the chance to escape.

These thoughts flooded my mind at the same time Jide loosened his grip on my throat and pulled down his pants. I immediately grabbed his scrotum, pulled, and squeezed with all the adrenaline that had flooded my system from his attack.

Jide let out a hellish yell that still resonates in my mind to this day. He fell off my body, kicking his legs in the air in spasms. His hands dropped by his sides as if he had fainted. When I gathered myself, I glanced at him—his eyes were rolling, and blood started trickling from his nose. Then, more blood spurted from his nose and mouth, and he stopped moving.

Realizing that Jide might be dead, I screamed at the top of my voice. Perhaps because the neighbors were in their own flats, nobody heard me, and nobody responded. I went to where Jide was lying on the floor in my room, half-naked. I shook him and called his name, pleading for him to wake up—but he didn't move.

I cried and cried until I was thoroughly exhausted, but Jide remained motionless.

Fear consumed me. Had I killed him by squeezing and pulling his scrotum? Panic set in. I tried to think, but my mind was a whirlwind of exhaustion and terror. The only thought I could hold onto was the need to run.

The moment that thought registered, I bolted.

I ran out of the gates of the compound. In front of the gate, I hesitated—I didn't know whether to turn left or right. Ahead of me lay the drainage system, now turned into a deep gully by erosion, the same place where I had once tried to drown before Mrs. Akinyemi rescued me. The thought flashed in my mind: maybe I should go now and finish what I started.

But as I considered it, I noticed several rough-looking men nearby, washing vehicles in the gutter. The water wasn't flowing that day because it hadn't rained.

Instinctively, rather than consciously, I turned left and kept running, sobbing as I went.

When I reached the main road, I turned left again, running and crying. As I passed people, they either looked bewildered, mocked me, cursed me, or simply stepped aside to let me pass.

I didn't know where I was going—I just ran forward, as I always had.

A few people made casual attempts to stop me, asking what was wrong, but I didn't give them a chance.

At one point, a police patrol vehicle pulled up, and an officer grabbed my hand.

"What is wrong?" he asked.

I kept crying, unable to speak.

After a few unanswered questions, one of the policemen in the vehicle scoffed.

"Officer, leave this evil girl. Let's continue our business. We can't waste our day on this kind of matter. Do you know what she has gotten herself into?"

They sped off.

I continued my aimless running, crying. People either laughed, mocked, cursed, or got out of my way as if they feared being "infected" by my troubles.

I ran all day, as if I was trying to escape from myself. From what, and to where, I had no clear idea—I just kept moving forward, as I always had.

By late afternoon, utterly exhausted, I stopped by a pavement under the shade of some trees.

I woke up with a start when I felt rough hands grab my left arm. I turned and saw a filthy, wild-looking madman with overgrown hair. His stench hit me, and I screamed at the top of my voice.

The madman, startled by my screaming, quickly let go. I sprang to my feet and ran with all the strength I had left.

Fear of falling asleep again—of that madman coming for me— kept me from stopping, even though I was weak, hungry, and faint.

I must have blacked out at some point because the next thing I knew, rain was falling on me. I heard horns blaring and opened my eyes to daylight.

I sat up and realized I was too close to the road, lying on the footpath. Slowly, I picked myself up and stumbled toward a nearby heap of sand, where I sat, dazed, watching the world pass by.

Then, the events of the last few hours flooded my mind.

So, I'm on the road again. On the run again.

Jide is dead—by my hand.

Mrs. Akinyemi didn't do anything wrong by taking me in, so how could I have killed her little nephew?

Like my father, I found myself crying out, "Ahhh, this life! Ahhh, this life!"

Just then, I noticed a dog trying to cross the road. A car hit it, killing it instantly.

That's what I should do, I thought. Get crushed and killed by a vehicle.

Without hesitation, I walked straight into the middle of the road.

But instead of the cars running over me, they screeched to a halt. Some crashed into one another in the chaos.

I stood there, frozen, as the commotion unfolded around me.

One furious driver jumped out of his car, marched over, and slapped me hard across the face.

"You witch!" he spat.

More drivers rushed toward me. Some were beating me, others cursing, shouting, and calling me names.

Through it all, I only cried, hoping they would do with their hands what their cars had failed to do.

Then, suddenly, I felt an urge to look up.

Through the mob, I saw a man walking briskly toward me. His eyes were locked onto mine.

I stared back at him.

Despite the chaos—the blows, the curses, the spitting—nothing else mattered.

Only the man coming toward me with steady, confident steps.

I could not understand it, but I kept my gaze on him and felt no more of the pain of my ordeal. When he waded through the crowd and reached the spot where I stood, he raised his hands and shouted for the crowd to stop. He extended his hands, and I grabbed them, mentally and physically clinging to him.

When he started moving away with me, the crowd instinctively parted for him, as if acting on an unspoken command.

As soon as I was free from the crowd, I loosened my grip on him and fled. I did not notice any effort on his part to pursue me. When I had run far enough, I turned to look back, but I did not see him following me. So I stopped and began walking—just moving forward, again, not really knowing where I was going.

Somehow, for that day, I did not think about dying again. I just continued walking. Night and day became the same to me; I no longer distinguished between them. As long as I could move, I kept moving. When I could no longer stand or walk, I collapsed and lay there until something—a passing vehicle, an animal, or even a person—woke me.

Many people have tried to help me, but I always made sure to give them no chance. In my moments of clarity, I would recall all the efforts to take me in and care for me, from Mrs. Akinyemi to everything that followed. Because of that, I have refused to stop for anyone or follow anyone home again. The most I have done is beg for food from places that sell meals or groceries.

I have walked through rain and sun, night and day, in cold and heat, without stopping—except when my legs could no longer carry me. I only look for food when hunger becomes unbearable, like the day you picked me up.

For as long as I can remember, I have been walking forward without looking back, not knowing where I am going. Has it been months? A year? I cannot say. I really do not know how long.

I have not bathed. I have starved for days until my body could no longer endure the hunger, and then I would start begging for food or picking up anything edible from the roadside, trees, or farms. I have been drinking water from borehole sales points whenever I spotted them in the distance.

I have slept in any empty space I found—some with a roof, some without. Many people have tried to take me home, and I have refused. Many who came to attack me ended up running away, shouting, "She is a mad woman! She is a mad woman!"

In the last week or so, I have refused to take any food or water, hoping to drop dead. But at daybreak that day you saved me in front of your office, the hunger and thirst became so unbearable that I did not even realize when I started begging for food—until you came along.

I must stop now. Thank you. And I think I should add goodbye.

I just need to end this life.

Think of it—I killed my mother. My father may have died in prison. I do not know the whereabouts of my little brother, James.

What is there to live for?

Chapter Nine

As continued by Mofe Makanjuola

Sarah stopped abruptly after her last question—*What is there to live for?*

I had been stunned beyond measure, listening to her story day after day for the last three days. She would share, including the sordid details of her horrible experiences, until both of us would be falling asleep while talking.

When she finally asked, *"What is there to live for?"* I was caught off guard. I could not respond immediately. All kinds of emotions had passed through my mind, body, and heart since the past three days I had listened to her.

I was jolted from my reverie when she called my name, saying—

"Mr. Mofe, by tomorrow morning, I must leave. It has been my best break in life to meet you. I have been in your home now for three days, and you have neither asked to have sex with me nor attacked me. While it felt great to know I could be this safe with you—a man—it also feels abnormal compared to the life I have

known for the last seven years. It is only wise that I leave. You do understand, don't you?"

Tears were now dropping involuntarily from our eyes. I could not understand it. But when I gathered myself, I ventured—

"There is much to live for, Sarah. I promised you that if you told me your story, I would tell you what is there to live for."

She turned that mysterious gaze on my face again. Looking me directly in the eyes, I felt as if she was boring a hole into my soul, searching for the thoughts and feelings buried within me. It was as if she could see right inside me. She maintained her gaze, and then I felt she was intrinsically asking, *Are you real, Mr. Mofe Makanjuola?*

"One thing you can live for, Sarah, is to start searching for your father, brother, and mother. Your father must have come out of prison by now," I managed to say.

"And do you think he would be happy to see me—the source of sorrow and pain for him and the whole family?" she asked.

"I have never been a father to know for certain, Sarah, but from what I learned from my own father, never seeing you again is worse than anything he has gone through."

"Really?" she asked.

"Yes!" I said with all the energy in my heart.

"You know what, Mr. Mofe Makanjuola? There is something to live for. Nothing would be greater than meeting that man—the

greatest man on earth—my father, Enoch. Even if he is mad, blind, lame, or in any condition, I must find him, my mother, and my brother, James..."

She trailed off abruptly.

What she said next caught me off balance.

"Take me and make me your servant. Give me my parents and brother."

Tears. Tears. Tears. Both of us were now crying uncontrollably.

I had never experienced this kind of sorrow in all my life. The truth in her words was undeniable. Yet, the weight of it all—the reality of what she had endured—was overwhelming for me.

Without thinking, I threw open my arms. She jumped from her seat and fell into them, and we wept even more. By now, tears were running down my cheeks uncontrollably. We held each other for what felt like eternity.

She clung to me, her head on my shoulder, holding me so tightly I feared she would squeeze the life out of my body—as if her entire existence depended on me. We just held on, as if nothing else in the world existed.

At some point, I started catching my breath, and I noticed that she was now breathing peacefully. She had fallen asleep in my arms.

We remained like that. I had never had a moment like this in all my life. It was peaceful, reassuring, and blissful. I secretly wished it would last forever.

The comfort of the moment must have truly overtaken me because I, too, fell asleep. We slept in each other's arms and did not wake until the morning sun pierced through my window, washing over my face.

When I realized how long we had been like that, I was slightly alarmed—but also happy. The thought of such a chance lasting forever returned to my mind.

I thanked God it was a Saturday morning. If it had been a workday, I would have failed to get to the office, as I normally woke up at 4 a.m. to beat the traffic buildup on the Third Mainland Bridge.

I said a silent prayer in my heart that all would be well with Sarah and me. Then, I gently shook her awake and caressed her hair. The touch roused her, and when she awoke, she appeared alarmed. Then she stopped, heaved a sigh of relief, as if saying, *Oh, it is Mr. Mofe Makanjuola, so no problem.*

She laid her head back on my shoulder, as if to say, *I don't want this dream to end.*

The scent of her early morning female body sent my senses into chaos. She felt my reaction and sat up with a start, looking me directly in the eyes with that piercing, unreadable stare.

My body, which had been highly warmed up, went cold under the weight of her gaze. It was as if she was saying, *Rein in that animal before it spoils the greatness of this moment.*

Then she smiled. She planted a kiss on my forehead and said, *"When I told you yesterday to take me, I really meant it. If you want to have your way with me, I will count it an honor."*

She cupped my face in her hands and held my head against her bosom. The man in me responded immediately.

Just then, I remembered the vow I had made—against premarital sex. I had promised myself to be different from the other men Sarah had encountered.

I took a deep breath and said, *"Sarah, I love my mother and sister very much, and I made a vow to respect womanhood—wherever, whenever, and however I meet them. I cannot take your virtue away."*

"Mr. Mofe, I have no virtue. I have been violated. I accepted such a life in my past, giving myself to men for protection and other reasons, though it never worked out for me. It was all a mere mirage."

"Sarah," I countered, *"stop. With me, your virtue is intact. Let's not go into that now. We have work to do. We must find your parents and brother. Let's start planning."*

"Before any plans, Mr. Mofe, let me cook you a meal. I felt very refreshed in your arms last night. If you still need sleep, go to bed now. In an hour or so, I will wake you when I have fixed something for us to eat."

"Thank you, Sarah. I would love to get a good stretch," I said, squeezing her hands.

Chapter Ten

SEARCHING for Sarah's parents and brother became the central mission of my life.

After a delicious meal of my favorite jollof rice, fried plantain, and stork fish, which Sarah cooked and served with much care and affection, we sat back at the dining table to discuss how to locate Sarah's parents and brother.

I could see from her face and piercing gaze that Sarah was both doubtful and hopeful at the same time. You can feel it—you know that kind of feeling when you have it. Conflicting as it was, I was determined to exhaust myself in finding Sarah's parents and brother or at least get to the point of learning what had become of them.

In the days that followed, I kept having this feeling that I was on a mission, and that helping Sarah and her family in this great— though undeniably difficult—undertaking was something I had to do.

"Mr. Mofe, how do we go about the search for my parents and brother? Who would we ask?" Sarah queried.

"Sarah, let's start with the name of where you come from," I said.

"I don't even know the name of the township we were residing in before it all started," she admitted.

"Hmmmm!" I retorted.

"What about the name of your parents' township or village?" I asked.

"I know that my father told me in stories that we hail from Sapele in Delta State. He spoke about his town with some pride, I remember. We visited my father's hometown once when I was a little child, but I have no idea where that is," she said.

"Sarah, would you try to remember the township where you lived with your parents? It's important. For example, during your primary school years, did you not know where your school was located? That might help," I suggested.

She thought for a while and then exclaimed, "Yeah, I know! Our school signboard read 'Ikere-Ekiti!'"

"We're getting somewhere now, Sarah. If we must, we will go there and research the court records. We are sure to get a lead or even meet them there," I said assuredly with a smile.

That seemed to comfort her, as she heaved a sigh of relief and smiled for the first time since the conversation began.

Almost suddenly, she turned and asked, "What if that fails? What else would you do, Mr. Mofe?"

"I have been thinking about it—backup plans and other options, Sarah," I responded.

"Have you heard about social media? You know, Facebook, Twitter, Instagram, Google Plus, etc.?" I asked.

"Which one be that ee?" she asked, puzzled.

"I don't know how best to describe social media to you, but I can say it's a new method of communication, relationships, and connection that uses digital technology. It enables people to chat in real time and share information and pictures with others, even if they're far away. You can use social media to share information and find out what's happening hundreds or even thousands of miles away—or even in other countries. It's magical, in African parlance," I explained.

"How can that help in the search for my parents?" she asked quickly.

"One Facebook post, for instance, could be viewed by a hundred thousand people within one to twenty-four hours. If I posted a small piece of your story with your pictures, someone who knows you or your family might see it, respond, and help us connect with them," I said.

"Ahh!! That would be wonderful. Let's do it now!" she shouted excitedly.

"We need to go to a cybercafé for that. It could be done on some phones called smartphones. I used to have one until two weeks ago when it fell out of my pocket while I was rushing into a bus on the Island. I may be able to buy another one soon," I said.

"Then, let's go to the cybercafé now!" she commanded.

"Yes, Madam!" I answered, trying to lighten the mood. "Meanwhile, Madam Commander, I recommend you go take your bath now, and I'll follow up after you while you do your makeup."

I was happy when her emotions shifted from the seriousness in her voice to amusement.

She sprang to her feet immediately, replying, "At your command, sir," as she gathered the dishes and took them to the kitchen.

It appears women dress better when they are happy. By the time I had dressed and came out to the sitting room, Sarah had put on her best outfit and was standing before the mirror, applying her makeup. She was gorgeous. I could hardly connect the Sarah I was looking at now with the one I had been with these past few days.

She had blossomed—so stunning! Her dress accentuated her curves, highlighting her alluring femininity—her flat tummy, hips that seemed to have a life of their own, shapely legs, and matching breasts pressing against the fabric as provocatively as could be. She was breathtaking.

I must have been staring at her for too long because she suddenly turned toward me. I could see a questioning look on her face, followed by a slight smile at the corner of her lips as she asked, "Mr. Mofe, is there a problem?"

I was caught off guard and began mumbling, "Em, em, no, no, Sarah. No problem. No problem. No problem…" unknowingly overstretching the words and exposing my excitement at her beauty.

"Em, em… the look on your face, Mofe! I don't know what to make of it. Can you explain that look?" she asked, clearly enjoying the situation.

Now, it was my turn to feel alarmed because I had been caught lost in thought, picturing her without clothes—though she was fully and modestly dressed.

"Er, er… no problem. I'm alright. Are you alright, Sarah?"

I doubt I convinced her because she smiled discreetly and then said, "Mr. Mofe Makanjuola, I hope I am safe ooo?"

"Ahhh! You are safe, my dear—very safe," I said, trying to muster as much bashfulness as possible. "You are also very beautiful."

"If you're ready, let's go," I added, making a great effort to mask the turmoil Sarah's beauty had stirred in me over the past few days in my house.

"Okay ooo. Let me just assume I am safe, and thank you for the compliments. I have not heard those words from any good man before," she added.

To maintain my composure, I stepped outside and waited for her to finish and come out.

We headed to the cybercafé not far from my house. She kept walking very close to me, and our hands touched several times. Instinctively, I grabbed her right hand with my left, and we walked like that for a short distance before both of us simultaneously realized we were getting rather too intimate. We quickly pulled our hands apart and then burst into laughter.

From the way we laughed, it was clear that we both understood what had happened but had also chosen not to acknowledge, at least outwardly, what was stirring between us.

Shortly before we entered the cybercafé, we realized—through a near-miss accident with an Okada—that we had joined hands again. We couldn't quite remember when it happened. Just as we were about to turn into the cybercafé, an Okada rider nearly ran us over and harshly warned, "Hey, you lovebirds! Una no go commot for road?"

Inside the cybercafé, there were quite a lot of people. A desktop was vacated by a lady who had just finished using it. With a sigh, she got up and walked away. I immediately sat down, pulled a nearby empty stool closer, and asked Sarah to sit beside me.

Before I could finish opening my Facebook page, Sarah asked for the third time, "How can this social media help me find my parents and brother?"

I gently tapped the back of her palm with my left hand, then grabbed and softly squeezed it. She heaved a sigh of relief, and I could feel her calming down.

Now on my Facebook page, she was stunned to see my pictures, friends, events, and several of my posts and updates. As soon as she saw it, she asked, "Can I get mine?"

"Yes, you can. It's part of my plan today. You can make posts, ask the whole world any questions you like, and get answers—sometimes annoying ones, some to laugh at, and others that are reasonable. It's like a freedom palace."

I took her picture with the webcam, uploaded it as a status update, and wrote the following message:

"My name is Sarah Enoch. I have been missing from home for about seven years now following a series of disasters that sneaked in without warning upon our family, stole our peace and serenity, landed my father in prison, caused my mother to lose her mind, left me wandering the streets I do not know for all these many years, and separated me from my only brother, James. I want to know where to find my parents and my brother James. Please help me. You can contact me through Mr. Mofe Makanjuola at 0812-599-9990. Thank you for your help."

I asked Sarah if she liked the composition before posting it for the whole world to see.

"Yes, it is very good, Mofe! You remember my story. I am touched in the deepest part of my heart. I owe you my life. I pray to God every day to bless you and grant you all your heart's desires."

"Amen, amen, amen," I responded.

"Now what, Mofe?"

"We'll go home now. If people who know you and your family see this post, they'll call my phone, and we can explore that further. We'll also check the Facebook post for comments and leads that could help."

"Oh, okay. Thank you."

I could hear the despondency in her response. It seemed she had expected some magic to happen right after the post.

I decided to take time to explain other possibilities—including the undesirable likelihood of the Nigeria Police Force coming after her for the death of Jide.

"Aahh! Mofe, that would be a serious problem ooo! Maybe we should remove the, the, the Facebook post ooo," she stammered.

"Well, Sarah, dear, it would still be a good thing for the police to be involved in finding your parents. If they come to arrest you for Jide's death, it would give you a chance to prove your innocence. From my little knowledge of human rights, you acted in self-defense. The law recognizes self-defense in matters like that. Being a woman, that would be easily understandable."

"Mr. Mofe, I am confused and afraid."

"Don't worry your little head, Sarah. It will all be well in the end," I said.

"Okay… if you say so, Mofe. I believe you."

"There's this song by Whitney Houston that says, 'There can be miracles when you believe.'"

"Music? Mofe, can you play it for me? Can you sing it for me?"

"Play, yes. Sing, nooooo. My voice would make you hate the song, hahahaha. When I get back my smartphone next week, I'll download the song and play it for you."

"Mofe, I would really like to hear your voice singing. For me, everything about you is soooo sweet. I get the feeling that if you sing, it would be sweet too. But if you don't want to sing for me… okay ooo."

"Sarah! I will sing for you one day. But right now, I do not see myself singing."

As we chatted along the road back home, I noticed Sarah became quite relaxed. The feelings of uncertainty and hopelessness that had clouded her earlier seemed to have lifted. She appeared happy, and that made me feel good.

Before we retired for the night, Sarah's anxieties returned.

"When did you say Facebook will tell me where my parents and brother are again?" she asked.

"Sarah, dear, I didn't say Facebook would tell you where your parents are. I said that if we post your story and picture on Facebook, someone who knows you and your parents might read about your story and help connect us to them."

"That doesn't sound real anymore. When you first told me about Facebook, I felt like it was the solution. Now, it's not. Mofe, is there any other way we can check?" she asked.

"There are other ways. We can go and report to the police. However, I do not trust the Nigeria Police. If we report your case to them, they'll put us under interrogation, and one or both of us might end up in trouble—or in prison. They lack the diligence to investigate cases, and they use detention as a shortcut to cover their ineptitude. I do not have any influential person in my family who could ensure we get out of it. Please have patience.

From my experience on Facebook, within three days, we should have a lead. There's a chance your father is already out of prison, has a smartphone, and even has a Facebook account. If that's the case, he could stumble upon your picture and story. I don't know for sure, but I have a strong feeling that our answer lies in social media—of which Facebook is the leader."

I tried to reassure Sarah.

Anxiety continued to build up in the house every day as Sarah worried about the delay in the miracle I had promised social media would bring. The whole situation gave me a new insight into the woman upon whom my heart had found a landing. I saw firsthand how edgy Sarah could be when things weren't going her way or as fast as she wanted.

Interestingly, instead of loving Sarah less, I started pondering how I could manage her oversensitivity during challenges and still love her. Each time I faced these thoughts, I laughed quietly at myself for being head over heels in love with a total stranger—who might even end up being a ghost.

On the third day, I felt a pressing need to get a new smartphone. It was becoming difficult to keep going to the cybercafé to check for updates, and I knew regular updates could help spread the news faster.

Since it was a Saturday morning, I excused myself, went to a nearby shopping mall, and bought a small smartphone.

As soon as I finished configuring it and logging into my Facebook account, a first response came in regarding Sarah's post.

It brought so much shock and happiness to our hearts all at once.

I couldn't quite understand it, but Sarah and I both felt a tinge of fear, shock, and overwhelming joy at the same time—especially after reading the message and discovering who had responded.

The response read thus:

Babajide Odumosu

"Oti o… yepaaah… this bad girl… so you are still alive? The police would hear this… bad girl… hahahaha!"

After reading the response to Sarah, she exclaimed, "Oh my God! When shall I have peace in this world? So Jide did not die? Now I don't know whether to cry or rejoice… whether to be afraid or happy. Ahhh! Mofe, is this a bad or a good omen? What shall we do?"

"Dearest Sarah, this is a good omen. Jide is alive! It's wonderful to know that you have no blood on your hands. Now, you also know that Mrs. Akinyemi won't have to live in regret for saving your life and caring for you when it mattered most. I feel we should rejoice rather than sorrow. This is a happy turn. I am now so confident that this project will work and that we will be able to connect with your parents and your brother one day soon."

"Mr. Mofe Makanjuola, are you trying to calm me down, or do you really feel this way?"

"Sarah baby, R-E-A-D M-Y L-I-P-S – I A-M H-A-P-P-Y-Y!"

Her eyes became teary. Then, without warning—but in typical Sarah spontaneity—she jumped at me. Because I was unprepared, we both came crashing to the ground. Thankfully, we were sitting on the couch, which saved us from a terrible happiness accident.

As Sarah smothered me in a bear hug and kissed my face all over, I inhaled the womanish scent of her well-perfumed body. The lingering fragrance from her nighttime bath, mixed with the warmth of her skin, washed over me, making me wish she would never get up.

We lay there for what seemed like an eternity—me savoring every trace of her scent and enjoying every moment. Then it struck me that if we stayed like this much longer, I might lose control. I tapped her back gently and said, "Sarah, we need to explore this Jide angle to see what we can learn. Perhaps more opportunities will open up through him and Mrs. Akinyemi."

"Mofe, are you sure I can face Mrs. Akinyemi after everything I did? As for that Jide boy, nothing good can come from his path," Sarah asked, getting up from my body.

"Yes, Sarah. This is not the time to be afraid. It's time to explore all possibilities—and, if necessary, all impossibilities—to find your parents and Brother James."

"I trust you, Mofe. I love you, Mofe. I will do whatever you say—whatever you want us to do in this matter. For everything about my life. So, what do we do now?"

"Let's reply to Jide's post and ask how we can meet him and Mrs. Akinyemi."

"Mofe, do it," she said without hesitation.

So, I responded to Jide:

Mofe Makanjuola

"Jide, good to have you respond to our post. Sarah and I would like to meet you and Mrs. Akinyemi to apologize."

His response came immediately:

Babajide Odumosu

"For where? Who wan see that dangerous bad girl again?"

Mofe Makanjuola

"There's something important, please. We need your help."

Babajide Odumosu

"Wetin? O.Y.O."

"Mofe, what is he saying?" Sarah queried.

"He's not agreeing to my request to visit him. Not yet."

"Do you think he ever will?"

"I think he will. It might take some time—some chatting—to convince him."

"What did he say last?"

"He said 'O.Y.O'—On Your Own."

"Tell that boy to be reasonable for once in his life," she said in a commanding voice.

"Hmmm… I don't think Jide will be persuaded by commands. We have to move gently. As our people say, it's gently-gently they use in licking hot soup."

"Okay, Mofe. Anything you say. You're the boss."

Once Sarah felt she needed to let me handle the conversation, I continued chatting with Jide.

Mofe Makanjuola

"Sarah would really like a chance to apologize to you and Mrs. Akinyemi, pleaseeeee."

Babajide Odumosu

"Hmmmm. Ok. I'll tell my aunty first. If she agrees, I'll inform you."

Mofe Makanjuola

"Oshe gan, my brother. I look forward to hearing from you soon."

"Well, Sarah, Jide has decided to ask Mrs. Akinyemi if she would agree to our visit. Let's wait for his report."

A now-anxious Sarah nodded in silence.

The room fell quiet for what felt like forever. Jide's response was the only straw floating on the water where we were drowning, and we held on to it tightly.

Then Sarah broke the silence.

"Mofe, even if we meet Jide and Mrs. Akinyemi, what help will it bring? Neither of them knows who I am or where I came from. I never had a chance to discuss those details with them. That poor old lady accepted me with all her heart—without judgment—which made me feel good. But if she had been able to find out more about me, that trip to her home… and that terrible Jide… ruined every chance. I can't see the help or the hope."

"Dear Sarah," I said with a tone of pride, "I took an investigative class in university as an elective in civil security. Investigators are trained to maintain a positive attitude and explore all options—no matter how insignificant they seem. In fact, I love chasing ridiculous leads in investigations, and I usually find great insights doing so. So, my friend, any lead to your past is a lead worth pursuing."

"Okay, my prince charming, thank you for always knowing what to say to calm my nerves. Every day, I pray for you. I ask God to bless you—especially for my sake. Apart from my time at Mrs. Akinyemi's home, being with you is the first time in years that I have felt like a human being... like I'm not worthless. Thank you, Mofe Makanjuola. I love you."

Before I could process what she was saying, she fell back onto my body and planted a kiss on my lips that left me stunned—holding it until both of us started melting.

Suddenly, she withdrew from the consuming intimacy and looked at me with a mix of guilt and burning desire, her mouth slightly open and inviting. To me, the look on her face announced that we were overstepping the bounds we had set, yet it also enticed me to go for it.

In a split second, I rationalized that she had told me to take her earlier, but I strongly felt it would be a huge mistake—one that could ruin everything. I summoned the last vestige of my moral strength, gently disentangled myself from her, held both her hands, and said:

"Sarah, I love you. I have been praying to God that our search for your family would end well—meaning, we would find them, and I would marry you."

"Oh! Really? You are praying to marry me one day? Oh, God, so You did not forget me! Thank you, Mofe. Thank you, Mofe."

She heaved a sigh of relief and fell back against my body, this time resting the back of her head on my chest. With teary eyes and muffled sobs, she prayed:

"Oh, God, please bless this one man who has proven to me that I am worth saving instead of destroying me further."

I was relieved when she finally sat up, brushed my hair with her left hand, and announced that she wanted to go and fix lunch.

That Saturday, we stayed indoors, with Sarah breaking into Pentecostal church songs from time to time.

By evening, she asked, "Have you checked if that Jide boy has said anything again?"

"No, he hasn't," I replied.

I could feel her anxiety rising from her tone. I reassured her that these things take time.

"There is even a chance that he has not been able to ask his aunty about the possibility of our visit, or he may not have data to come online to respond," I said. "And Sarah, please don't let your anxiety take over. I have this superstitious belief that if one is too anxious about something, it's a sign that it won't come out well. This is a time to trust God, not to be anxious or afraid."

"God forbid!" she shouted. "It is not my portion. This thing must work out, ooo. Mofe, this thing must work out, ooo, please."

"It will," I said. "I need it to work, ooo. I want to use its success as bait to win your love and make you marry me, hahahaha," I added, trying to lighten the atmosphere.

"Can you imagine?" she blurted out. "Mofe, you are not serious, ooo. What kind of talk is that? We are discussing something serious here, and you are making jokes."

"Sarah, let me tell you—I am a smart guy. Only a fool would see an angel and let her fly away. I am using my entire arsenal—my brain and my prayers—to ensure that you are mine forever."

She must have sensed the matter-of-factness in my words from the tone of my voice. She stopped, looked me piercingly in the eyes, heaved a sigh of relief, and said:

"Mofe, you make me want to forget my ugly past. The God who blessed me with you must also bless you for me."

She started singing some of those church songs again.

I went into the bedroom, took a pillow and a blanket, and came back to the sitting room.

"It's time to go to bed now," I announced. "Since your arrival, you've been sleeping on the couch in the sitting room. You are my guest—you should sleep on the bed from today forward."

"I'm sorry, Mofe, but I shouldn't be sleeping on the bed while you, the owner of the house, sleep on the couch. Apart from that, you are older than me and, therefore, appropriately my senior brother," Sarah replied.

"I feel that you are worth more," I said. "I just want to be sure I am taking appropriate care of you. I get this feeling that you sleeping on the couch makes you less than me. So, I insist that you sleep on the bed, and I will sleep on the couch to remove my guilt."

"Mofe, dear, there is no way I am going to sleep on the bed while you sleep on the couch. It doesn't seem right to me. Moreover, what would people say if they found out about this situation?" Sarah declared.

"Sarah, I don't care what people say. My decision is my decision, and I am old enough to carry my cross and its consequences," I said.

Sarah, in her usual way, looked at me directly in the eyes, questioning. Then she said, "Come ooo, what is the idea? If this is so you can sneak in beside me while I am fast asleep, that doesn't sound smart at all."

"Come on, Sarah! Me, sneak in on you? What's the purpose of that? Now, that's a dumb conclusion, girl! What do you take me for?" I asked sarcastically.

Sarah, not one to be beaten easily in an argument—though clearly out-reasoned this time—turned the tables on me by saying:

"Mofe, the only way I am going to sleep on that bed is if you sleep there with me. On this couch, I can control my emotions since I don't have much room to move. It helps me keep my body together. But on that cozy bed of yours, the moment I turn in my sleep and feel a wide space, my body will ask to be cuddled."

"Sarah, you are impossible. Did we not agree that we would not get involved in sexual intimacy unless we are married? I don't want to sleep on the same bed with you unless and until I achieve my goal—which is to find your family and make a good woman of you—my wife!"

"So, Mofe, I am not a good woman unless I am your wife, right?" she said, giggling. "Ahaa! Mofe, now we are talking about family and marriage. I don't even know anything about you except that you are a good man—good enough to want to save a lost girl. Tell me about you," she said.

"Well, Sarah, family for me consists of my mother and sister. There are just three of us. I didn't get to know my father the way you knew yours. He was said to have died when I was just a child, and my younger sister was still unborn. My mother single-handedly raised my sister, Damilola, and me. She never remarried.

The first time I noticed, as a growing boy, that my mother was struggling to provide food, clothing, housing, and education for us, I made a vow that day: I would work hard to make my mother proud and to be a good boy—to help my mother and my sister."

By the time I realized that I had been looking down, squeezing my palms tightly, I looked up and saw that tears were now streaming down Sarah's face. She was staring at me with such consuming intensity.

Tears flowed from my eyes in response.

As our eyes met, Sarah opened her arms and nodded for me to come into her embrace. Without hesitation, I virtually fell into her outstretched arms, and she held me so tightly, rubbing my back and stroking my hair with her left hand—an act that brought both great comfort and an undeniable awakening of my manliness. The bliss was out of this world.

We just held each other without speaking. I clung to her as if to say, *Please, do not go away.*

For a moment that felt like forever, we ignored the riot playing out in our bodies. While my manhood stretched to its breaking point, Sarah started breathing rapidly. Involuntarily, she began parting her legs, a rhythm I instinctively responded to by pressing my body closer and closer to hers.

To our horror, we both simultaneously reached for each other's casual daywear. As soon as I pulled down the narrow sleeve of her dress, exposing one of her succulent breasts and moving toward it with my mouth, she gently tilted my head with both hands and asked, "Is this the right time?"

Horrified, I lifted myself off her body.

"Sarah, I am sorry. I was carried away. Your tears were so healing, comforting, and inviting, and I know those are real tears of kinship. I love you, Sarah Enoch.

"You and I have come a long way in life. I now believe that everything you endured—your pain, your abuse, and your ordeals—led you to find me. I owe you. I want to honor you with the highest honor a woman can receive from a man. I want to make myself worthy to be your husband, to have you, your parents, and James, your dear brother, accept me as a member of your family. And I want to do so on a bed undefiled," I said.

Our tears flowed profusely but without sobbing.

"Mofe, I love you with every breath, every fiber, every drop of blood, every vein—with my whole being. You have some magic that I want to live with for the rest of my life. It is incredible how one man can erase the bitterness and bile I have built up over the last seven years.

"I am beautifully shocked that, despite my own personal desire and willingness to become your sex toy—something every other man in my life has forcibly made me—you are preserving me, talking about making a good woman of me, giving me hope. Oh, God! I do not want to lose this magic or the man behind it—Mofe! Please, dear God, grant me this one thing," she said, half-speaking, half-praying.

Spontaneously, we both used our fingers to wipe each other's tears. Then, we burst out laughing, disentangling ourselves and sitting there, savoring the wonder of the love we had just witnessed and felt for each other.

Then, Sarah burst into laughter again. She got up from the seat, laughing harder while eyeing me with that coy, sexy playfulness of a girl in love. She took a few steps away from me.

"Sarah, what is it now?" I asked.

"Mofe, I just erased one naughty thought that had been on my mind since I came to your house."

"What is it?" I asked.

"Please accept my apology for judging you wrongly. They call it prejudice, I believe. At first, when you wouldn't attack me for sex, even pulling away when I made advances, I thought you weren't man enough. Each time you talked about marrying me, I feared you might be impotent or unable to get your penis to work.

"But while we were locked in that deep, intimate bliss of an embrace, I felt your manhood rise—big, rock-solid—and I felt completely wet, pouring out my fluids," Sarah said.

Horrified and elated, I shouted, "Whaaat! This girl, you are crazy ooo! You're lucky you ran away before saying this; otherwise, you'd have been in hot soup. Can you imagine the nonsense you were harboring in your mind? Well, sorry to disappoint you, ladylove, but I have standards. Part of that standard is the honor I have deep in my heart for womanhood.

"Remember, I was raised single-handedly by a woman. I have a younger sister who is about your age now. They mean the world to me. You mean the world to me. I would never do anything to dishonor the great women in my life."

"Mofe, to be honest, at first, I was confused as to why you didn't want to have sex with me. At one point, I wondered if it was because of my past—if you were afraid of disease. But then I remembered that most of the men who took me in wasted no time at all, and there were opportunities for you to take advantage of me before you even heard my story.

"Now I know that I have met a real man—a man of his word. They call it 'a man of integrity.' Now I know that because of the love you have for your mother and sister, you vowed to honor other women.

"Thank you for including me in your honor roll."

Sarah blew me a kiss from her fingertips and vanished into the bedroom. Moments later, I heard running water. A few minutes later, she emerged in her nightgown and announced that all intruders to her sleeping couch should vanish immediately; otherwise, they would be liable for breaking their vows.

I had no choice but to reluctantly go into the bedroom to get some sleep.

I lay awake most of the night. I wasn't worried about sleep not coming—tomorrow was Sunday, and I didn't have to hurry to work like on weekdays. I kept thinking about this enigma called Sarah.

I thought about many things. I thought about how a wicked and uncaring world could have destroyed such a great soul like Sarah because of its cruelty and indifference. I thought about everything she had been through, and my soul grew weary that such wickedness pervades our world.

As if I needed even more time to think deeply about Sarah, sleep refused to come.

I thought about the possibility of marrying her, whether we found her parents or not. I feared how my mother and sister would react to her circumstances. I worried about the condition of her parents and what impact that could have on our marriage.

Despite these fears, everything about Sarah felt right in my heart. The more I considered my fears, the more I felt reassurances from an unknown place.

At some point, I was scared—what if Sarah wasn't who she claimed to be? What if I was wrong to believe her story and take her into my house without fear? What if she turned into something else—a wild animal or a malevolent spirit—and devoured me?

But as I wrestled with these thoughts, they always ended in a feeling of peace—*all will be well.*

I thought of better ways to continue the search for her family. Many of them didn't seem easy to coordinate with my work and daily life. But I kept having the strong feeling that our contact with Jide and Mrs. Akinyemi would lead us to success.

I was deep in this reverie when I heard:

"Mofe, Mofe, Mofe! Wake up. It's daybreak. Let's get ready for church."

At church that day, I really did not listen to the sermon. I spent my time contemplating the way forward with Sarah. She noticed that I was completely distracted and gave me questioning glances several times.

When we returned home, she asked without waiting for us to settle down:

"Mofe, what happened at church today? Your mind was not there at all. It got me worried. Are you wondering how long you're going to put up with me?"

"Come on, Sarah, don't even think about that. There's nothing wrong with me, and I'm not worried about anything, so don't worry your little head," I lied.

"Well, dear Mofe, if you must know, I love you so much, and I feel that my heart is intertwined with yours to the extent that if you so much as feel anything, I feel it immediately. The difference is that I may not fully understand the feeling right away, but deep down in my soul, I do feel whatever you feel. And when you are worried, I get worried too. So be smart and start telling me what's wrong, or this great home that has felt like heaven in the last week or so will suddenly feel too small for our voices."

In the time I've been with Sarah, if I've learned anything, it's how highly intuitive she is. I also admire her ability to discern things and, of course, her skill in speaking her mind without hesitation when necessary. For me, I hesitate over many things, but Sarah does not. Instead of being scared by this trait, it made me admire her even more.

"Alright, alright! You're right. I have been worried since yesterday. I hardly got any sleep last night. Even when you woke me up, I realized I was daydreaming about my worries and thoughts instead of sleeping."

Sarah walked over to where I was standing, placed her hands on my shoulders, pulled me close, and said:

"Mr. Mofe Makanjuola, look me in the face and listen. When you told me there is something to live for, I didn't believe you. But your kindness gave me the strength to hold on. As soon as I was able to share my traumatized life story with you, I started believing in the possibility of something to live for. So, I shared mine with you. Pay your dues—share your worries with me. I am an angel. I will take your worries away and hand them over to God to solve."

As I looked at Sarah intently, imitating the way she usually looked at me, I felt peace. I shared with her that I had been worried because Jide had not responded to our last request to meet with him and Mrs. Akinyemi. Tomorrow is Monday, and I need to be at work. I had hoped that by this weekend, we would have made some progress with Mrs. Akinyemi.

"Oh, oh! See me see trouble ooo! This reminds me of once upon a time when my mother was so worried about other people's problems, and my father called her 'the dancer who dances more than the owner of the ceremony.' Oh, Mofe, are you now getting more worried than me?"

"It's not that, Sarah. It's just that I'm worried you might abandon me if we don't get results fast."

"Ahhh! Ehen! Good one. It seems one guy is in love with a total stranger wanderer he picked up on the road and calls an angel!"

"Well, Mofe, I'm so happy I was picked up off the road by you. I'm grateful. On that fateful day we met under such bizarre circumstances, one of the feelings I got early on—which I fought hard to dismiss and why I quickly took off—was: 'Sarah, take this rescue line and hang in there until I fix all things for you.' I didn't believe the voice. I was afraid of all my past experiences and didn't want anything to do with anyone again."

"I believe now that God was speaking to me that day. I know now who the real angel is—his name is Mofe Makanjuola. 'I have been touched by an angel,' just like that movie we watched two nights ago."

"I was actually going to ask you what has become of that naughty boy Jide's promise to help. One part of me told me to be patient before asking."

"Sarah, they call that being sensitive to other people's feelings and challenges. Thanks for your sensitivity and care. Sometimes, I feel like we've known and loved each other all my life, yet it's only been a few days."

"So, Angel Mofe, is there anything we can do now about this Jide boy's nonchalant attitude?" she quipped, giggling.

I felt reassured like a baby by her response, and I almost started to behave like a child in love. I was so happy, and it probably showed because she then asked, "Who is happy there?"

I dared not answer because it would be impossible for me to hide from the truth, which I didn't want to admit.

"Yes, Sarah, I want to send him a new text and update my page on the search. You never know when someone with knowledge will be online and see the post."

"What are you waiting for?" she asked.

I picked up my phone immediately and sent Jide the following message on Facebook Messenger. The conversation unfolded as follows:

Mofe Makanjuola:

"Hi, Jide! How are you doing? I haven't heard from you since we discussed Sarah."

Almost immediately, Jide replied:

Jide:

"Mr. Man, do you think the only work I have is to worry about that bad girl, Sarah?"

Mofe Makanjuola:

"No, no. I'm only pleading for your help."

Jide:

"Mr. Man, if that girl do you something, you go see ya-self. Be careful ooo."

Mofe Makanjuola:

"Please, Jide, try for my sake."

Jide:

"Wetin be ya own sef for this matter?"

Mofe Makanjuola:

"Jide, my brother, Sarah needs help. I know you care about her enough to help her, don't you?"

Jide:

"I no care for that gal. She is dangerous. But you, Mofe, you don too worry me. I go tell my aunty now that that dangerous girl is still alive. Those days, she used to worry and cry about her. I don't even know why anybody would love and care for that dangerous girl you people call Sarah."

Mofe Makanjuola:

"Oshe gan. Thank you, my brother. I will be waiting for your response."

"Sarah dear, you must have done something really bad to that guy. Hahahahaha. He doesn't want to hear anything about you. He never told Mrs. Akinyemi anything, but he's promised to do so now. Let's keep our fingers crossed."

"Oh! That Jide boy. Everything I felt about him the first day I set eyes on him has come to pass. I felt both unsafe and insecure in his presence. I also felt jealous that I would have to share Mrs. Akinyemi with him," Sarah said.

"Ahaaaa! Sarah, you are the cause of everything. Job in the Bible said, 'What he feared most has befallen him.' Because of your fears and hatred towards him, see what you're getting. Consider what could have happened if you had loved him…"

"Love him? That boy? Have you ever seen him and how hateful he is?" Sarah cut in.

"Sarah! Hush! Once bitten, twice shy," I interrupted. "Don't spread your hatred for him again, so we don't hit a roadblock."

"Okay ooo! Whatever you say, Mofe. You're the boss."

"Wow! Sarah, it's 10:15 p.m. It's time to go to bed. I have to leave for work early tomorrow morning."

"That's true, Mofe. Sorry for taking too much of your time."

She dashed into the bedroom, took her night shower, and returned to the sitting room with her nightgown, wrappers, and pillow.

The next morning, as early as 4:00 a.m., I was awakened by sounds coming from the kitchen. I got out of bed and went straight there—Sarah was already up, preparing a meal.

"Good morning, Mofe. I hope you had a good night's rest," she asked.

"Good morning, Sarah. Yes, I did. How about you?" I replied.

"Oh, I slept well, Mofe. I woke up with a start around 3:00 a.m. because I saw you in a dream lamenting that you woke up late and were running behind for work. I decided not to go back to sleep but instead to do some chores and prepare breakfast for you before you leave. I had planned to wake you at 4:00 a.m. so that by 5:00 a.m., you could eat before heading out."

"That's very thoughtful of you, Sarah, but I'm not accustomed to eating in the morning before work for a couple of reasons. First, I never have time to prepare food before heading out—I have to beat traffic. Second, I always wonder if it's too early to eat at the time I usually leave for work," I explained.

"Well, Mofe, that's about to change. Go take your bath and get ready. Let's make a bet: If you're ready before I finish making breakfast, you can leave without eating. But if I finish before you, then you must eat before heading to work today. Deal or no deal?" she challenged.

"Deal!" I accepted and left for the bathroom—hoping and praying she would both win and lose, as I wasn't sure how I felt about eating so early in the morning.

She won.

For the first time since I started living alone, I had a highly stimulating breakfast of fried plantain, scrambled eggs, and a hot cup of chocolate before leaving for work.

Throughout the day, I found myself singing—both aloud and silently. More than three of my colleagues asked what was making me so joyful or if something was wrong with me. Some even insinuated that I might have been bitten by the love bug.

Chapter Eleven

As told by Sarah Enoch

Some strange visitors came calling this evening. Their mission scared me and nearly ruined the romantic evening I had planned for Mofe.

After Mofe left for work that Monday morning, I busied myself cleaning and washing everything in the house that needed attention—his clothes, the bathroom, the kitchen, the bedroom, the sitting room, windows and doors, the front yard, and the backyard. I noticed many of his neighbors staring at me suspiciously, some in wonder, as if they were saying, *Who is this girl staying with Mofe? When did she come?*

I also overheard some talking about me admiringly, making gestures to indicate they were discussing me. Others showed signs of disbelief, while some looked visibly unhappy. Throughout the time I worked outdoors, I felt like I was being observed, either with admiration or curiosity.

From the sniffing, sneering, excitement, and awe I noticed on several of Mofe's neighbors' faces, it was clear that many were surprised, angry, or unhappy to see me—or perhaps just to see a woman in Mofe's house. Whatever they felt, I felt happy to be *the one,* though I couldn't quite explain why.

I kept myself busy throughout the day and didn't have much time to worry about anything. My soul was at peace with Mofe—his kindness, his trust, and the love I could sense from him, even though he hadn't spoken or expressed it as often as a woman would like.

A little after midday, I finished my chores. I dressed a little better than I had while cleaning and went to the Mallam's fruit market at a nearby junction. I bought some healthy-looking papayas, mangoes, and watermelon, made juice from them, and stored it in plastic jars in the fridge.

I still remember how my mother used to prepare special meals for my father from time to time. As I prepared the juice, memories of her treats for him filled my mind, and I began to wonder about my father, my mother, and James. What had become of them? The thought made me moody for a while.

Then I remembered Mofe had assured me that he would do everything in his power to find my family. That promise gave me courage, strengthening the confidence I had in him and the love I felt for him. I pulled myself together and continued reviewing everything I had to do that day.

After gathering myself again, I felt an urgent need to take a bath. I went to the bathroom, took my time, and took care of myself. Afterward, I sat in front of Mofe's standing mirror in the bedroom, carefully applying makeup—just enough to look cute but not overdone. I liked what I saw in the mirror and felt happy with myself.

It was now 4:00 p.m., and I started yearning for Mofe to return home. But when I realized that even if he left the office at 4:00, Lagos traffic would still delay him, I grew anxious. Then, realizing what emotions were passing through me, I laughed long and hard at myself, thinking, *Maybe it's not only Mofe who is falling for a total stranger in this house.*

I must have been lost in thought for too long. I was suddenly startled when electricity was restored, and the television came on loudly. I realized with some worry that we hadn't turned it off the last time the power went out.

The sudden noise made me glance at the wall clock—it was now 5:30 p.m. Time to fix dinner.

It wasn't going to be much work. We had Egusi soup from Saturday stored in the freezer. Since the power had been out for most of the day, it had fully defrosted. All I needed to do was warm it and make some gari. As I set the dining table, it occurred to me to add some flowers to make the evening feel more romantic.

I dashed outside and plucked some red, yellow, and blue flowers from the compound. While doing so, I noticed one of the men I had seen earlier in the morning while cleaning. He was now standing with another man I hadn't seen before, positioned directly opposite Mofe's door at the other end of the compound.

Our eyes met, but almost immediately, all of us looked away.

I went inside, set the flowers on the dining table, and arranged the room for Mofe's return.

However, I realized with some unease that I kept thinking about the man outside whose eyes had met mine. I couldn't understand why I was so bothered by him, but thoughts of him kept flashing in and out of my mind. Worrying thoughts—ones I couldn't quite grasp—kept creeping into my system, but I dismissed them each time.

By 6:30 p.m., it was time for my favorite television program. I tuned in and quickly forgot about the man outside who had been lingering in my thoughts.

Just as the 30-minute program was wrapping up, I heard a knock at the door.

I looked up at the wall clock—it was a minute to 7:00 p.m. *That's about the time Mofe returns from work,* I thought.

Excited, I sprang to my feet, adjusted myself, and peeped through the eye hole, ready to open the door as romantically as I could.

To my horror, I saw two faces.

One of them was the man I had seen outside earlier.

Instead of flinging the door open as I would have if it were Mofe, I hesitated and asked, "Who is there?"

A coarse voice answered from the other end: "And who are you? Where is Mofe? Is he not back from work yet?"

My heart skipped a beat. Then I muttered, "Yes, he is not back. And who are you?" I queried further.

The voice ignored my question and never uttered another word. I watched through the peephole and saw the people moving away from the door. I heaved a sigh of relief, only for a sense of foreboding to flood back into my mind. I sat on the sofa, wondering who they could be and whether I was in any danger. I must have been deep in thought when I drifted into a reverie. Another knock on the door—this time gentle and recognizable as Mofe's—recalled me to reality.

I peeped through the peephole again, and to my relief, I saw Mofe. Though I could see other heads behind him, I was not as frightened and worried as I had been the last time. I opened the door and was about to fling myself at Mofe when he gave me a look that silently pleaded for my understanding. I took the hint and stepped aside to let Mofe and the two visitors enter the room.

Both men were older than Mofe. One was clearly over fifty, with gray hairs rimming his head, while the younger one appeared to be in his late thirties.

Without invitation, they immediately threw themselves onto the three-seater sofa. They started almost in unison:

"Mofe, is this why we didn't see you at the town meeting last Sunday?"

"Mofe, Mofe, does your mother and sister know that you are now living with a woman in your house without marriage?"

"Na your clear eye be this, or she don bewitch you?"

"Talk now, ooo. Let's know when to act to save you from danger."

"Have you forgotten that you are an only son and that your poor mother and sister are depending on you?"

"You don forget say, for our culture, we no dey permit people wey no marry to live together?"

The questions kept rolling out, one man speaking in proper English while the other spoke in pidgin.

Mofe stood there, bemused, a look of concern on his face. When they finally paused, he stammered, "Ehm! Ehm! Uncle Bode, it is not what you think."

"If no be wetin we dey think, then, Mofe, wetin be this wey we dey see here?" the older man pressed. "I hope you no forget say you be my sister's only son. When Bosun call me today come talk wetin he saw for your house this morning, I said, hmm, I must come and see before I go believe. Now I don see am for myself say woman dey your house. For me, ooo, you don reach to marry, ooo. But you must do it well well. Your late father marry my sister well well. I marry my own wife well well. We no dey do kurukere thing for our family. So wetin you say dey happen here, Mofe? You don tell my sister about this?"

"Uncle Bode, it is a long story. But I want to assure you that we are not doing anything wrong. I want to assure you that you raised me well. When my father died, and you took us in and helped my mother to find her feet again, I saw how you lived with your wife and my cousins. I secretly vowed that I would copy your family's lifestyle of love and respect for your wife, your children, and the people around you.

"So, Uncle, please understand—Sarah is not here because I have forgotten my training but because of the circumstances in which I found her. I decided to help her find her parents and brother again. When I heard her story, I felt a sense of duty to help. I promise you, her stay here is temporary. And if it ever becomes more than that, I will do it the right way—with you as my father, standing before us."

"Mofe, you don speak long grammar. However, you don become man now. I no suppose push you around. My own na to advise. But I must tell my sister, ooo. Make you no count am say I don do you bad and report you to your mama. But you must understand say I cannot keep quiet for this kind of thing wey I see for ya house today."

As I stood there listening to all this, tears started flowing from my eyes. I was stupefied. Palpable fear came over me. I worried for Mofe and for myself. I did not know what to think or say.

Then I remembered that Yoruba people—Mofe's tribesmen—expected young people to bow or kneel when speaking to elders. I lowered myself to my knees for the rest of the conversation.

I noticed that as soon as I did, Uncle Bode turned to look at me. His expression softened with a hint of kindness or sympathy.

When Uncle Bode finished speaking, he stood up. Mofe said, "Uncle Bode, please wait. Let us bring water and food before you go."

In a much lighter mood, which comforted me, Uncle Bode replied, "Mofe, when you marry, you can invite me to come eat for your house. Me, I no fit eat for bachelor house. I no wan eat food wey I no know who cook am. Any day wey me I know say you don marry, I go come eat for your house."

Uncle Bode then turned to me and said, "Woman, I hope say you hear everything wey I don talk. The reason wey I dey struggle to speak broken English is so that you will hear me. When we talk Yoruba to Yoruba, we no dey mix grammar. Me, I no dey hide my feeling, ooo. Mofe is a good man. Be careful wetin you dey do with him or wetin you dey plan. I no dey quarrel with you, ooo, you hear?"

"Yes, Uncle," I said, bowing even lower to the ground.

Both men stood up and left. Mofe followed them outside the compound. I stood at the door, watching until they had completely left the premises. I heard their car start, the doors slam shut, and then Mofe walked back through the gate toward the house.

I remained at the door, frozen. I did not move a finger until Mofe returned. He met me there, still standing as if blocking his way. But I wasn't. I felt as though my world was collapsing again. My limbs were too weak to move. I cannot recall how long I stood there.

I only came back to reality when Mofe gently placed his hands on my shoulders. In his gentle, reassuring voice, he said, "Sarah, don't worry yourself to death. There is no cause for alarm."

"Really, Mofe? Really?" I muttered. "Your uncle does not approve of my staying here. Can't you see that?" I thundered.

"Yes, I assure you," Mofe responded. "There is no cause for alarm. Couldn't you tell that he only disapproves of us staying together as an unmarried couple? Did you not notice that he is already taking a liking to you? Did you not hear him say that he is not quarreling with you? I know my uncle very well. I lived with him for many of my growing years. He loves and teaches with a kindness I have never seen in any other man to this day. He does not control people's lives; he helps them make wise choices on their own. He did not have much formal education, but he is the wisest man alive in my reckoning. He just wants us to act with wisdom. I think I understand his worries.

"Can you not now confirm my training and the way I have tried to live with you since we met, despite all your beauty, the sexual attraction, and all the sweet moments we have had together—without intimate sexual intercourse? May I come in now, sweetheart?" he concluded.

Reluctantly, and reasonably reassured, I stepped aside and let Mofe into the room.

The dominant thought in my mind was to sit down and ask Mofe to explain how he meant that there was no cause for alarm. Then, another thought flashed through my mind: *Why don't you welcome him home first? He might be just as much in shock as you are.*

I heaved a sigh of relief and said, "Oh, Mofe, sorry for all of this. As you can see over at the dining table, I had prepared a special evening to welcome you from the stress and strain of today's work and the Lagos traffic. Look at the dining table, but first, go into the room, freshen up, shower if you want to, and then come over to get some food, which I have poured all my love into preparing for you."

"Ahaa!!! That's my girl. Thank you. I'll be with you shortly," he said as he made to rush into the bedroom, then stopped short, turned, grabbed me, held me tightly, and planted a kiss on my forehead.

In that moment, my mind went wild with expectation—I thought he was going to get down with me. In the speed of light, I decided to go along with it. Then, he let go of me and dashed into the bedroom, whistling.

As he whistled and rustled about while bathing, I reflected on the whole evening—my fears, my tears, and then the light of hope that came with the warmth of his bear hug and forehead kiss. I felt relieved and heaved a big sigh of relief.

When he was ready for dinner, he came into the living room beaming with a satisfied, confident look on his face. I wondered why.

As he approached the dining table, I expected him to move to his side and sit down. But instead, he came over to my side and held out the chair for me. I looked at him with deep affection mixed with consternation and managed to quip, "Mr. Mofe, which one be this now?"

"Sarah, please take your seat. That's what great and important guys do for their ladies at the dinner table. Did you not see it in the movies?"

"Oh, so you are learning to act in movies with me, hey?" I asked.

"Sarah, sweet, please take your seat. This meal was prepared with much love and affection, and I want us to eat it with commensurate love and affection," he said.

"Hmmmmm! Somebody is spoiling somebody ooo. If anything 'bad' happens after all this love, nobody should hold me responsible ooo," I said as I sat down, feeling cozy.

Before he could leave my side, I stretched out my hand and rubbed his neck.

He drew his chair to the other side but sat close beside me instead of across from me, as we had always done before.

We ate with a warmth I had never experienced in my life. I was practically glowing, and he noticed.

"It seems someone is enjoying this meal more than me ooo," he teased.

"Before nko? Mofe, if you knew what you were doing to my body, maybe you would be wise to stop now before—" I started saying before he cut in.

"Sarah, sweet, what is it that I am doing to your body that can cause trouble?" he asked.

"Well, for your information, young man, I am a grown woman. My body has taken over the joy you have planted in my heart… Ahh!! I can't explain what I am feeling right now. It is better felt than explained. My whole being is on fire. Please help me," I said, gazing helplessly at him.

"Errrr!!! Sarah, dear, I am just trying to compliment your great cooking, your thoughtfulness, and your care. You care as deeply as only one other woman I have known in this world—my mother. Please be at peace. I am happy, and I can't hide it."

I sat speechless, my lips probably hanging open. He picked up a piece of dried fish and placed it on my lips. I grabbed his hand and took both the fish and his fingers into my mouth, sucking hard at them.

He stood up, moved closer to me, and held my head to his chest. Expecting him to bend down and kiss me, I let go of his hands. But he jumped back and said, "Sarah, I had in mind that after dinner, we would try to see what Jide got for us."

"Ahhhhh! Don't be a spoilsport. That's the last name I want to hear in this great moment we are having," I said, confused and a little angry.

I was embarrassed and not embarrassed at the same time when he said, "I'm sorry if I have aroused in you emotions we are not ready to express now. I was aroused too, and I had to run before I capitulated."

"Wow! What kind of man runs when a woman already desires him to take her?" I asked.

"I am Angel Mofe. That's what you called me the other time, isn't it? Or better still, I am Joseph in Egypt. I would not be the first to do that," he said.

"I hope nobody is calling me Potiphar's wife," I said, feigning anger.

"No! No!! No!!!" he said.

"Hmmmm! Mofe, I love you. I wish this moment with you would never end."

"Same here, beautiful," he said as he started eating.

We ate mostly in silence, glancing at each other like young lovers deeply lost in affection.

After dinner, Mofe got up first and exclaimed, "This is a beautiful experience—eating with an absolutely angelic being. Thank you, Sarah sweet," he said and started clearing the table.

"Wow! So life can be this beautiful," I muttered as I stood up and joined him in packing away the dinnerware and storing the remaining food in plastic bowls for the freezer.

When we had cleared the table, I deliberately stepped into his path, grabbed him with both hands, pulled him to my chest, and planted a peck directly on his mouth.

"Thank you, Mr. Mofe Makanjuola," I said, letting go of him and turning toward the couch to sit down.

To my surprise, he grabbed me, swept me off my feet, planted a kiss on my forehead, and gently set me back down. He followed me as I walked away.

In that fleeting moment, my mind raced to the bedroom, my heart pounding at the thought that we might finally be heading toward some steamy sexual intercourse, given the charged atmosphere of the dinner.

I was slightly disappointed and, at the same time, highly elated when he gently put me down and nudged me toward the couch in the seating area where we usually lounged together after meals.

I had grown to believe that whatever a man does for a woman is ultimately to get her into bed. I also wondered what the right kind of compensation for his kindness would be. With that terrible mindset—that all a man wants is sex—and with no idea how else a woman can return love, I had thought that sleeping with Mofe would be the best way to show my gratitude.

On the other hand, I was elated that he was not after sex with me and that his declarations and displays of love and affection were genuine. Though I did not personally feel worthy, Mofe made me feel both worthy and whole. It was thrilling that a man like Mofe— young, handsome, and educated—would consider someone like me deserving of all that he bestowed upon me. I silently prayed that if this were a dream, I would never wake from it.

We reached the couch and collapsed together, tangled in each other. Though I did not feel any pain from his left hand brushing against my shoulder, I clutched it and let out a muffled scream.

"You've wounded my shoulder!" I cried.

He quickly adjusted himself, caressing my shoulder with soft apologies. That gave me the perfect opportunity to lie fully on his body, which was exactly what I wanted. For some time now, we had been ending up this way every night after dinner—either watching TV or discussing random topics until sleep overtook us.

"I didn't even have time to ask how work went today. Your uncles rattled me so much that I forgot," he said. "So, how was your day?"

"Todaaaay? At work?" He drew the words out dramatically, flashing a suspicious smile. "Hmmmm. I don't think I want to talk about it."

"Oh, oh, oh! Don't tell me you met another 'traumatized angel' at work today and plan to bring her home to replace me?" I teased.

"Hahahahahaha! I'm so happy someone is jealous of her angel Mofe being taken over by another. That makes me feel highly desirable and important."

"Me? Jealous? Impossible. Try someone else with that one!" I fired back. "How can I be jealous? What's my own in this?"

"But jokes aside, Mr. Mofe Makanjuola, I'd really like to know how work went. I want to be sure you were okay. I need to know that the breakfast didn't make you sleepy on the job or cause any problems," I said in my usual matter-of-fact tone.

"Calm down and let me talk," he chuckled. "When you start with 'Mr. Mofe Makanjuola,' I know the jokes are over. So, your royal majesty, queen of my heart, you won't believe what happened today. I'm both excited and embarrassed to share it."

"Share it! Share it now! No more beating around the bush!" I urged impatiently.

"I was singing at work today. Either singing out loud or humming a tune. My colleagues even noticed and started asking if I had won the lottery or if something was wrong with me. The intuitive ones shocked me by saying they suspected I had been bitten by the love bug."

He paused, grinning. "The truth is, your breakfast this morning was superb. It's been a long time since I had eggs prepared like that. When I make them, I can never get rid of the raw egg smell. But this morning, my body rejoiced with that meal, and it affected my soul—so much so that my soul sang out, sometimes without me even realizing it. In my village, they would say you gave me love juju."

I couldn't stop myself from clapping and shouting, "Wow, wow, wow!" Then, jokingly, I added, "'Angel Mofe,' what really happened to you? Would you mind telling your mother what you got yourself into?"

Mofe roared with laughter, playfully smacking me. When he finally gathered himself, he said, "This woman! If I don't get you, you'll get me. There's no escape."

We both burst into laughter. Then I turned and looked at him intently, as lovingly as I could. I opened my arms, and he practically ran into them. We held each other in a tight embrace until our bodies responded with dangerous warmth, and we quickly pulled apart.

Mofe, always skilled at changing the subject when things got too heated, suddenly said, "Aha! Sarah, sweet, we need to check on Jide now."

"Yeah, I reckon we should. But please, don't bring Jide into our lives when I'm savoring your love and kindness. He's bad omen, remember?" I said.

"Sarah, sweet, please stop. In this house, only one person hates Jide—you. As for me, I love him."

I pulled away and looked at him in shock. "How can you love Jide and also claim to love me?" I demanded. "Something doesn't add up, Mofe."

"Okay, okay, no wars," he said, raising his hands in surrender. "Let me explain. If you had gotten along with Jide, where would I be now? So, for me, Jide is my greatest ally. His foolishness ensured that I would be here today, savoring the presence of an angel. Can you process that, Sarah, sweet?"

"Goodness me! That is a terrible joke," I scolded. "Mofe, are you well at all? Can you even hear yourself? That's horrible! But anyway, let's get in touch with that scoundrel and see what he's up to."

Mofe was now laughing so hard that he collapsed onto me. He grabbed his phone, opened his Facebook account, and suddenly screamed, "Yeah! Yeah!! Yeah!!! Listen to what Jide wrote!"

Jide Odumosu

"Hey! Mofe, the juju that bad girl gave to you and my aunt na very strong one, joo! She dey sing and dey praise God since she heard that that bad girl still dey alive and wan come back to her. She say any day wey una wan come, make una come quick quick."

When Mofe read that message from Jide, tears started rolling down my cheeks. I didn't know if they were tears of joy or something else. I felt as if we had already found my parents. My hopes and fears were mixed together.

I stood up, looked lovingly at Mofe, and opened my arms wide in front of him. He had since come to know what that meant. He came without hesitation, arms stretched. We closed in on each other, and I practically hung on his neck and sobbed. He rocked me until I fell asleep standing, hanging on his body in that spot. The next thing I realized was when he swept me off the ground, laid me on the couch, went into the bedroom, fetched my wrapper, nightgown, and net, placed them near me, and then went to bed.

The hope kindled by meeting Mrs. Akinyemi was so overwhelming. Though I could not fathom how meeting her would help my cause, I was nevertheless filled with hope and some relief.

When I woke up early in the morning—before 4:00 AM, when I had set the alarm to wake me up daily to make breakfast for Mofe—I remembered that we had not responded to Jide or made concrete arrangements for when we should see Mrs. Akinyemi. So, I went and woke Mofe up.

He looked at the time on his phone and complained, "Hey! Sarah Sweet, it is not 4:00 AM yet."

"Yes, I know, Mofe. But remember, we didn't respond to Jide, and we didn't make arrangements or inform him of when we might visit and get their address," I said.

"Ah! Yeah! That's true," Mofe responded, still half-asleep.

I watched him stretch in his pajamas. I could still smell the perfume he had applied after his bath the previous evening before that memorable dinner. I admired the contours of his body, visible even through the fabric.

He is quite handsome, I thought to myself. When he stood up, I saw that his John-Thomas was also standing erect, pushing hard against his pajamas. I muffled a laugh, quickly looking away. He noticed where my attention had been, muffled a laugh of his own, then turned away with some embarrassment and asked me to leave the room while he used the bathroom.

Mofe must be a great man with integrity and discipline, I thought to myself. He has that JT that other men would be flouting—so agile and strong, as I have felt it several times—and yet he is resisting a sexually knowledgeable, active, and willing woman who cannot resist him. This one, Mofe, is the real deal, the real man, I concluded. Where had he been all these years of my travail?

A few minutes later, he joined me in the kitchen. He said he had replied to Jide, thanked him, and wanted to know whether I preferred Saturday or Sunday for the visit. I thought the earlier, the better.

"Mofe, if Saturday is okay for you, let's give them Saturday morning," I said.

"Okay, great. I will tell Jide now and await his response and confirmation of their address."

"Thank you, Mofe."

"Anytime, Sarah Sweet," he said.

"Mofe, go and take your bath now. I'm making you breakfast. Is it safe to make you breakfast?" I asked, teasing.

"Yes, Sarah Sweet. Why do you ask?" Mofe asked.

"I don't want to hear that someone is dancing reggae in the office today instead of working," I joked.

"My goodness!" Mofe exclaimed. "You are terrible! You finished me! I won't eat breakfast unless you beg me properly."

"What do you mean by 'proper begging' now?" I asked playfully.

"You'll see when the time comes. I'm going to take my bath now. You'll see when the time comes," he repeated.

Before he was done bathing, the breakfast—beans, boiled plantain, and fish stew—was ready. He preferred having breakfast before dressing and brushing his teeth so that no oil would drop on his work clothes. When he was ready to eat, I joined him at the table.

Just as he was about to start eating, I reminded him that I hadn't begged him yet. He sat back, laughed, and said, "Oya, beg me now, or I won't eat this food."

"Mofe, eat ooo. Time is not on your side. Don't just sit there waiting to be begged."

He acted as if he was about to get up but was only pretending.

"Please, please, my lord, eat your breakfast so that you can sing all day and not work today, hahahahahahaha!"

"Whaaat! That is not acceptable begging," he said.

"Okay, I have an idea. You must not reject it," I said.

"Go ahead," he said.

I scooped a spoonful containing a piece of fish, plantain, and some beans into my mouth, walked over to him, took his head in my hands, pressed it against my breasts, then gently tilted his head and fed him from my mouth. He took it and ate. When he could finally speak, still with some food in his mouth, he shouted, "This is more than I asked for, ooo! But it is mmmmmmm! Sarah, you are baaaaaad! Go away and let me eat my food in peace."

I was happy to watch him leave the house glowing that morning. He kept glancing back as I stood at the door, watching him leave the gated compound where we lived.

"Oh God, keep Mofe safe for me. Grant him a great day at work. Bless him to be happy. I love him," I prayed softly as I closed the door and re-entered the house.

Chapter Twelve

MOFE returned home late that evening from work, whistling. He was obviously happy and called out before I could even greet him.

"Sarah, sweet, I have good news for you! Jide, your friend, responded to say that his aunt is ready to meet us on Saturday morning. I don't know why I'm feeling so confident about this meeting providing us with the key to finding your parents..."

"I know why you're happy about the meeting," I cut in. "You can't wait to see your partner in crime, that nasty Jide boy."

"Oh, Sarah, sweet, you won't stop fighting with this Jide boy, eh?"

"Well, I don't want to welcome you with a fight. So please, come and let me hug you welcome."

With my arms spread wide open, I welcomed him into my warm embrace. He virtually flew into my arms, and we clutched each other tightly. I pecked him on the cheek and bid him welcome. We held onto each other as we squeezed our way to the bedroom, where we allowed ourselves to fall onto the bed.

I disentangled myself, took his handbag, and placed it on the cabinet. As he proceeded to undress, I announced that his bathing water was ready and that dinner would be hot and waiting by the time he was out of the bathroom.

He started whistling—*this kind of girl, I never see am…*—as he always did each time we reunited peacefully when he returned from work.

Mofe believed that since my description of Mrs. Akinyemi fit an elderly, well-traveled person, there was a chance she might know where people from my hometown and state might be residing in Lagos.

I also discovered that I had reasonable peace of mind and lots of hope about getting ahead in the search for my family through Mrs. Akinyemi.

However, as I thought about meeting her, I felt both fear and shame for what I had done—putting her in some trouble and running off without the courtesy of getting back to her all this while, only to reach out when I had a need of my own. I prayed earnestly for comfort and peace of mind for both her and myself.

From time to time, the thought of apologizing to Jide would flash through my mind, but I would quickly reject it—sometimes doing so aloud.

At some point, Saturday seemed so far away. I worried from time to time. On one of those days before Saturday arrived, I was in one of my worry-induced moods while we were both at home.

Trust Mofe—he seemed to be completely into me and always noticed those moments when I was lost in thought. In his sweet, gentle way, he would barge into my stream of thoughts.

"Sarah, sweet, what is it this time?" he asked.

Embarrassed that I wasn't able to hide my feelings as well as I thought, I looked down at the floor and muttered incomprehensibly, "I…I…I'm alright."

"Well, if I didn't know you, maybe I would agree that you're alright. But given that I live right inside your heart and occupy all the space in your whole soul, I know what you feel and think at all times. So, Sarah, sweet, talk to the grandmaster of peace and happiness, and I will give peace to your soul and plant happiness in your heart," he boasted, as he always did.

"Hold me, Mofe. I keep getting worried that Mrs. Akinyemi will judge me as a bad sort, given all the trouble I put her through and my failure to get in touch since then."

Instantly, Mofe stretched his hands toward me, and I gratefully fell into those hands—hands that had wiped away my tears and soothed my sorrowful heart many times since our auspicious meeting.

As he held and caressed me, I clung to him tightly, as if my next breath depended on him. As always, I was restored, and I let out a sigh of relief.

Planting a peck on his lips, I said, "Thank you, Mr. Mofe Makanjuola."

Then, gently and reluctantly, I pulled away from him.

Ultimately, Saturday came. As if Mofe were going to work, I woke up at 4:00 AM to prepare.

Mofe said, "Sarah, sweet, please get some sleep. Saturdays don't have as much traffic as weekdays. We'll be okay leaving the house at 9:00 AM and should reach their place in good time. If not for a market we have to pass before getting there, the journey wouldn't take long.

"From the address Jide gave me, Mrs. Akinyemi lives at Meiron Estate, not far from Abule Egba Junction. Since we're in Iyana Ipaja, we're not too far from them. We're on the same bus route."

I said, "Okay, oo, but I'll keep getting ready *small small.* And I want to make sure we have a meal before leaving the house. My mother always made sure we ate together before leaving on Saturday mornings. Oh, my mother…"

Tears misted my eyes as I thought about the wonderful mother I once had, whom I had sorely missed for the last seven years.

I stopped short as tears started streaming down my cheeks uncontrollably.

My sudden silence caught Mofe's attention. He woke up, came over to me, held my hands, and started squeezing them.

"Is it about your mom?"

"Yes," I said.

"Well, you can't lose hope now. We'll visit Mrs. Akinyemi today, ask a lot of questions, and through her, explore more opportunities to find your family. Please, have faith. And above all, know that I am here with you until the work is done, okay?"

"Thank you, Mofe. You are truly an angel. You remind me that regardless of what I've been through, God still cares for me. Meeting you, Mofe, is my testimony that God lives. Thank you. Thank you, Mofe."

He took me into his arms, and I felt peace as I rested my head on his shoulder while he gently rocked me.

The time was 8:30 AM. The sun was already blazing.

The large, enclosed compound was calm. There was no early morning hustle and bustle like on a normal weekday.

As we opened the gate and stepped onto the road, I saw people moving back and forth and vehicle horns blaring. Though the roads weren't as congested as on a weekday, there were still many vehicles—long and small buses, taxis, and some fancy cars.

In my mind, there were just too many vehicles on the road at the same time.

"I thought you said there would be no traffic today, Mofe?" I asked.

"Hahahaha!" he laughed. "Do you call this traffic?" he asked. "This is no traffic, ooo. When you see Lagos traffic, every vehicle will be at a standstill, and even human beings will fill the whole of this road, brushing against each other as they pass. Iyana Ipaja is a busy area in Lagos. Before we finish this journey today, you will see some real traffic—don't worry," he concluded.

We crossed to the other side of the road, walked to a nearby bus stop, and took one of the small buses. I had experienced Lagos noise, traffic, crowds, and blaring horns before, but I had never gone through what I was about to on this bus ride. The last time I was on a bus, I wasn't paying attention to the flow of traffic since I had no idea where I was going.

Several times, we were held up by vehicles stopping right in the middle of the road to pick up passengers or by trucks and buses stuck in one of the many ditches at the center of the road, unable to move. From Iyana Ipaja to Meiran doesn't seem like a long distance, but it took us more than an hour to reach the Meiran Bus Stop, where we alighted.

In my opinion, Lagos traffic is caused by a combination of too many vehicles, too many people, terrible roads, and reckless drivers who have no problem stopping in the middle of the road to pick up passengers.

At Meiran Bus Stop, we saw several multi-story buildings painted the same color, their roofs showing signs of aging. People and vehicles moved in and out of the main gate. Mofe took the pedestrian side gate, and I followed him. As I stepped into the huge arched entrance, my heart skipped a beat. To my left, I saw a collapsed drainage system with a thatched shade built over it. The sight jolted a memory—of the massive drainage system eroded by heavy rainfall and speeding floodwaters, the very one I had nearly jumped into before Mrs. Akinyemi called out to me that fateful day.

A sudden fear gripped me. We were close—too close—to Mrs. Akinyemi's house.

All the positive self-talk I had used to prepare myself for this moment vanished. I had planned that the moment I saw her, I would fall flat on the ground, cry, beg, and call her "Mammy" until she lifted me up as a sign that she had forgiven me.

"Mofe, Mrs. Akinyemi's house is not far from here—I can feel it," I whispered. "And this thatched shade on the left, I remember it well. I slept there the night before and waited out the rain. It was here that I saw the flood filling the drainage system, rushing past with terrifying speed. I was about to jump in when the kind Mrs. Akinyemi called me back and took me into her home."

"You must be right, Sarah, sweet. Jide said their house is the second building from the gate on the right."

As I turned from the thatched shade, I recognized the building instantly. My body froze. I stood still, staring at Mrs. Akinyemi's house.

The next thing I knew, Mofe was screaming and yanking me back as a vehicle nearly hit me.

"What were you thinking, standing in the middle of this busy estate road?"

I just stood there, dazed. Mofe held my now trembling hands and gently guided me toward the house.

Mrs. Akinyemi's flat was the first one facing the entrance within the block of flats. As always, the front of her house was cleaner than the adjacent one. Her flowers were still blooming, even though it was the dry season.

By this time, my heart was pounding against my chest. My breathing quickened. Mofe noticed and squeezed my hand to soothe me.

"Sarah, sweet, calm down. Mrs. Akinyemi will be happy to see you again. You have no idea the mental torture she might have gone through after returning and not finding you. Seeing you today might be a great relief for her. So, please, dearly beloved, calm down."

I turned and looked at Mofe with all the affection I could muster. Moving closer, I clung to him as if, without him, I would sink into a raging river.

"Thank you, Mofe, dear."

He squeezed my palms in acknowledgment and then knocked on the door.

"Who is that?" came a voice from inside the house—one I could never mistake. That awful Jide boy. Oh God, is he the first person I have to meet today? I wondered.

Still holding my hand, Mofe replied, "Ehh, Jide, my man! It's Mofe Makanjuola. I'm here with Sarah to see you and your aunty."

The next thing I heard made my fear mix with anger.

"So, that evil girl Sarah is still alive! True, true! Oh God, why do good people die while those who should perish still live?"

At that moment, I heard Mrs. Akinyemi call out to Jide.

"Olajide! Olajide!! What is going on there? Why are you speaking such words this morning?"

"Aunty! It's that evil girl, Sarah. They are here."

"Stop that nonsense and open the door for them immediately! Be reasonable for once—you're no longer a child. Tell them I'm coming right away."

Jide opened the door and ushered us in. He stood by the doorway, scanning me from head to toe with the same hateful glare

I had always known him for. As our eyes met, I made sure he felt an equal hatred from me.

Closing the door behind me, he turned to Mofe.

"Mr. Mofe Makanjuola! You are strong, ooo! You've been staying with this evil girl, and she hasn't killed you? In just two hours alone with her, I met my ancestors! If not for the fact that they didn't want me back that day, I wouldn't be standing here. Some people here are more wicked than me," he concluded.

"Jide, my man, I hail you. You are a great guy. Thank you for welcoming us to your home and for the great work you did to help us come here to apologize to you and Mrs. Akinyemi."

"Apologize to this animal boy?" I snapped.

"Sarah, sweet, please don't go there. Allow bygones to be bygones, please."

"Mofe, you see am? Shebi I been tell you the kind of evil girl you dey deal with. Be careful. And don't say I no warn you."

At this point, Jide locked the door, offered us a seat, and sat down at the other end of the room, a little far from us, as if he wanted to make sure he had no connection with me. I was equally happy about that, as I could not stand him.

The room looked well-kept, with a sweet fragrance as always. There were still live flowers growing in flower stands in the four corners of the room. I had learned a lot about keeping rooms clean and tidy from Mrs. Akinyemi during the time I spent with her before that evil Jide boy came calling.

Just then, Mrs. Akinyemi emerged from the direction of her bedroom.

She looked as radiant as ever—just a little aged, and it appeared as if her gray hairs had increased. But she looked stately and healthy.

Mofe and I stood up instantly, as if we were conjoined twins, except that Mofe also prostrated for Mrs. Akinyemi. I stood there, fixated on the spot, speechless.

Just then, it seemed like a fresh breeze entered the room and beat against my face. My eyes opened as I gazed at Mrs. Akinyemi and noticed that tears were running down her cheeks. At this point, I collected myself, fell to the ground, and started sobbing.

"Mammy, I am sorry! Mammy, I am sorry!!" was all I could mutter.

She bent over me and picked me up from the ground.

"Sarah, dear, I am thankful to my Creator that I can see you again. My heart has ached every day since I returned from that trip and learned what happened. I had feared the worst but have also prayed every day that the good Lord would keep you safe. Welcome back home, sweetheart."

As she spoke, I clung to her and hung on her body as if my life depended on her. Tears continued to flow. She held me lovingly and stroked my long hair. In her embrace, my composure returned, and a peaceful feeling swept over my whole being. I sighed, releasing the pain and anguish that had weighed me down.

When we disentangled and she led me to sit beside her, we noticed that Mofe was still kneeling. Mrs. Akinyemi called him over.

"Thank you, my son, for saving this angel," she said, giving him a hug.

The three of us sat on the long sofa, with Mrs. Akinyemi in the middle. The sight was restoring to my soul—the two people dearest to me at this moment, sitting with me.

"Oh, God! I thank you for this great moment in my life. Please help me meet my parents and little brother James so that we can all sit together like this soon."

All this while, Jide sat away from the rest of us, obviously sulking. Childishly, I felt happy that he seemed excluded and unhappy.

Mrs. Akinyemi burst into song—*O God, Our Help in Ages Past*—as she got up.

"Sarah, my angel, please come with me," she said.

I got up and followed her to the kitchen. As I left, I rubbed Mofe's hair, filled with love and appreciation for his perseverance and commitment to embark on this journey with me.

"I delayed having my breakfast so that we could all eat together when you arrived. Let's bring out the food so we can eat together."

"Oh no! We ate before coming out. When we were small, my mother always made sure we ate together on Saturday mornings before leaving the house, no matter how early she wanted to leave."

"Sarah, you both are going to eat again. Nobody rejects food from their mother. You are my daughter, aren't you?"

"Of course, Mammy. I am glad to be your daughter. The life I have in me today, I owe to you. So, you are my mother in every sense of the word."

"By the way, who is the young man with you? Are you married now?"

"No, Mammy! It is a long story.

"He picked me up one day when a crowd of rowdy boys and girls were beating me up, thinking I was a mad young girl. I don't remember how many months I had roamed the streets without bathing, food, or a place to stay since I ran away from this house. That fateful day, I was so hungry and faint. Though I had prayed to die and thought hunger would help kill me, for some strange reason, when I noticed a woman frying akara, yam, and plantain by the roadside, I went to beg for food.

"That was when the boys and girls swarmed me, beating, flogging, and throwing stones and whatever objects they could find at me. Then I heard a voice shouting at them, calling some of them by name, and asking what I had done to deserve such treatment.

"I looked up, and our eyes met. It felt like salvation was in his eyes and hands. Instantly, he came down from the upstairs where he was, dismissed the boys, and asked me what my problem was. I pointed at the akara on the table in front of me.

"He bought some for me, and I collected it, thanked him, and started walking away before he ran after me, practically turning me around to face him, and asked me to tell him my story. After my efforts to dissuade him failed, I followed him back to his office and then to his home after work that day.

"When he heard my story and my desire to reunite with my parents—if they were still alive—he said he would help. I have been with him since then, and we have been searching for my parents.

"When he posted my story on Facebook, Jide replied, and they had been conversing until Jide finally agreed to help us meet you again.

"We are here for two reasons—first, to apologize and to see you again, and second, to see if you could give us a lead to trace my parents, as I do not remember much about where we lived when misfortune swept me away from the warm embrace of my parents and little brother, James.

"All I know is that our school signboard read *Ikere Ekiti* on it."

"Oh! Wow!! That's a great young man there. I hope what I am feeling happens to both of you. He would make a great husband. He reminds me of my husband, Joseph Akingbola Akinyemi. He was such a devoted man who would sacrifice everything to make me happy during our dating and courtship and throughout our marriage. I miss him."

I felt this kinship that only women can understand with Mrs. Akinyemi and the kind of marriage she may have enjoyed. I moved closer to her and hugged her with all the emotion and intention I could muster. She stroked my hair again and said, "Everything will be alright. It always is with men like Mofe." I was comforted.

Mrs. Akinyemi and I returned with the food and set the table. I had never seen such a rich breakfast in all my life. It was an assortment of delicately prepared dishes—fried rice, plantain, moi-moi, pap, beans, raw tomatoes, tomato sauce, omelet, and fish.

We laid out the table and invited Mofe and Jide to come over.

Mofe got up and looked toward Jide, who was not getting up, so he hesitated. He then gave Jide an encouraging look before dragging himself up. *That guy cannot behave himself at any time,* I thought.

Jide virtually dragged himself to the dining table. Mofe put his hand behind him and practically goaded him to the table. Mrs. Akinyemi noticed his foot-dragging and called him out.

"Olajide, what is your problem? Is this not your chance to apologize to this young lady you tried to assault?"

"Aunty me, I dey come," Jide replied.

"Jide! How many times must I tell you to stop speaking broken English in this house?" Mrs. Akinyemi queried.

"Sorry, Aunty me," Jide replied.

"Jide, it is not 'sorry, Aunty me.' It is 'Aunty, I am sorry,'" Mrs. Akinyemi corrected.

"Okay, Aunty. Thank you," Jide said.

"That's better," Mrs. Akinyemi added.

A subdued Jide was the person who sat at the table with us. Mrs. Akinyemi said grace over the food, and we ate mostly in silence. Jide was jittery throughout. He kept throwing glances at me and turning his face away each time I tried to meet his gaze.

To my surprise, Mofe and I ate much more than I expected, considering we had already had breakfast earlier. The meal was warm, delicious, and too inviting to resist.

When the meal was over, Mrs. Akinyemi and I started gathering the dishes. Mofe came and joined us. Jide looked at him with awe before coming over to help pick up the plates.

When I tried to start washing the dishes, Mrs. Akinyemi stopped me. She said I shouldn't worry about that for now so we could have time to talk about my parents. Jide had told her that I wanted to know if I could trace my parents through her.

"After learning from Jide that you and this young man would be making this trip here to find your parents, I remembered that you once told me you could only recall that your father hailed from Sapele in Delta State. Am I right?"

"Yes, Mammy," I said.

"There is a gentleman who resides in this estate from Sapele. Mr. Edewor lives with his wife, children, and elderly mother, with whom I have exchanged pleasantries often. I told myself that if you came around, we would go see them to find out if they could be of help."

"That is good, Mammy," I responded.

"Okay then, if you're ready, let's go and see him and his mother to find out if they can help."

Mofe and I automatically jumped to our feet at the same time, looked at each other, and smiled shyly. Mrs. Akinyemi noticed.

After instructing Jide to take care of the house, we stepped outside. She took my hands, drew me close, and insightfully noted, "It seems that you and Mofe are deeply in love."

Timidly, I nodded in the affirmative.

"He is a good-looking young man," Mrs. Akinyemi said. "I hope the two of you are careful to avoid problems?"

"Yes, Mammy. Thankfully, he is more careful than I am. He is such a golden-hearted man. There are times I feel I should offer myself to him for his love and kindness. Each time, he nicely refuses and refocuses me on something else," I responded.

"Wow! His type is rare in our decadent world today. Well, my dear, I must tell you that Mofe is demonstrating a long-misunderstood truth—love is different from sex," she said.

"Hold him tight through fasting and prayer and by ensuring you help him with house chores and meals. The best route to a man's heart is through his stomach—and good behavior," Mrs. Akinyemi counseled.

"I will, Mammy. He has given me a reason to live. Hopefully, I will find my parents, and maybe—just maybe—he might ask me to marry him, to which I would jump six feet in the air to accept," I replied.

"I know the feeling, my dear Sarah. I am praying for you. I am here for you. Now that we have reconnected, make sure we stay connected," Mrs. Akinyemi said kindly, squeezing my hands.

Mr. Edewor lived a few blocks away from Mrs. Akinyemi's house. After squeezing my hands, she stopped and looked back. Instinctively, I joined her.

Mofe was some distance behind us. *Smart guy!* He must have sensed that Mrs. Akinyemi and I were having an intimate woman-to-woman talk and decided to slow down to avoid eavesdropping.

"This is Mr. Edewor's apartment. Let's wait for Mofe to catch up with us. That young man is wise. He must have thought it right not to listen to our conversation and slowed down his pace," Mrs. Akinyemi observed.

"I thought so too," I said. "He is damn smart. I hope I can meet his standards."

"You are enough, my dear. The few days I stayed with you, I knew I was in the presence of light. The devil was just too jealous of you—that's why he tried to throw a thousand wedges in your path to destroy your greatness. Believe me, you are as smart, if not smarter. Just wait for things to fall into place," Mrs. Akinyemi reassured me.

As Mofe caught up, we turned into a block of flats. The Edewors lived on the second floor.

"Let's go up," Mrs. Akinyemi said.

We followed, with Mofe coming behind me.

Mr. Edewor's home had modest furnishings in the living room. However, it was dainty and welcoming. The room smelled fresh, as it looked clean.

Mr. Edewor received us at the door. Seated in the living room, where we were ushered in, was an elderly and equally elegant lady. She looked older than Mrs. Akinyemi. I thought to myself—this must be Mr. Edewor's mother. I was right.

"Good afternoon, Mama Edewor. Good afternoon, Mr. Edewor. Peace be unto this house," Mrs. Akinyemi greeted.

Mofe bowed to both Mr. and Mama Edewor. I joined him in curtsying.

We settled down as seats were offered. Mrs. Akinyemi thanked them and said, "We are here to seek your help. This young woman, Sarah, is searching for her parents. She said that her father is Mr.

Enoch, and they were residing at Ikere-Ekiti some seven years ago. That's the only thing she remembers.

Her story is a long one, and there is no possibility of starting that story here and now. Since you are from Sapele, I was hoping that, by chance, you might know or could lead us to find Sarah's family. This young woman has suffered more than anybody her age in this world. I hope you can help."

"Which part of Sapele is your father from?" Mr. Edewor asked.

"I don't know. The only thing I know is that my father once said, when I was nine or ten years old, that we are from Sapele.

I lost contact with my parents over seven years ago when my father killed a schoolteacher who raped me when I was eleven years old, and he was sent to prison. My mother lost her mind following my father's imprisonment, and my younger brother, James, and I were sent to live with my mother's elder sister, whose husband and son continued to rape me until I got pregnant.

When my aunt learned what had been going on between her husband, her son, and me, she said she did not want to see me in her house again.

I wandered the streets of places I did not know until Mrs. Akinyemi saved my life the day I wanted to jump into a gutter with a fast-moving flood. She took me in. My stay with Mrs. Akinyemi was short-lived because a little nephew of hers attempted to rape me.

I hit him so hard that I thought he had died, and I had to run away before Mrs. Akinyemi returned from her trip to the village.

I wandered the streets of this place I now know as Lagos until Mr. Mofe Makanjuola took me off the street some five weeks ago.

I just want to see my father, my mother, and my little brother, James, again."

"What a pathetic story. Do you know your father's surname?" Mr. Edewor asked.

"No," I answered.

"Given that the information available is scanty, this will be hard. I moved to Lagos only two years ago, so I don't know much. But I will take this to the Sapele and Urhobo Town Unions here in Lagos. One way or another, someone must know about a Sapele man residing in Ikere-Ekiti.

The Urhobo Union meeting is next Sunday, and the Sapele Town Union meeting is in two weeks' time. If you have a phone number, I will call you as soon as I have information. You can also take my number and call me from time to time as a reminder."

"Mofe here has a phone. He can provide you with his number and take yours," I said.

"Yes, yes," Mofe added.

Mr. Edewor and Mofe exchanged phone numbers.

Mrs. Akinyemi got up, thanked Mr. Edewor and his mother, and Mofe and I followed suit as we left.

As we walked away, my hopes were rekindled. This appeared to be a great lead, and I checked that with Mofe.

"Mofe, this meeting feels meaningful to me. I get a feeling that somehow, we will find my parents soon, once Mr. Edewor has checked with the Sapele and Urhobo Unions in Lagos," I said.

"I feel so too, Sarah," Mofe added in his usually reassuring voice.

As soon as we returned to Mrs. Akinyemi's home, she called out to Jide.

"Ahaa! Jide, where are you? I did not see or hear you apologize to Sarah for that foolish act of yours that led her to run away from here."

"Aaaah! Aunty mi, is she not the one who should apologize to me? She nearly killed me."

"Jide, why would she apologize to you? She did not do anything to you. She was only defending herself and protecting her pride. You are the one who attacked her and should be the one apologizing. I want to hear you do that now."

"Ok! Ok! I apologize," he said offhandedly.

"Olajide, which apology is that? To whom did you apologize?" Mrs. Akinyemi asked, sneering at Jide.

"Aunty mi, that girl nearly killed me if not for Mr. Chude, your neighbor, who heard me screaming when I returned back to life. And—"

"And so what, Olajide?" Mrs. Akinyemi interrupted him angrily.

"Eh! Eh! Jide, I am sorry for hurting you badly that day. Please forgive me," I said, hoping to forestall a major problem between Mrs. Akinyemi and Jide.

"Olajide! Olajide!! Olajide!!! How many times did I call you? Did you learn how to apologize, even though she does not owe you one? She was only defending herself and her virtue from a vulture," Mrs. Akinyemi interjected.

Now totally embarrassed, Jide managed to apologize properly.

"Ehm! Sarah, I am sorry for what I did to you. Please forgive me," Jide said.

Trying to restore normalcy, I said, "Apology accepted. Thank you."

"Ahaa! Sarah and Mofe, please sit down so you can at least get a drink and so that we can review our meeting with the Edewors," Mrs. Akinyemi said.

As we sat down, Mrs. Akinyemi offered us fresh orange juice and water. While placing the cups before us, she said, "I feel that our visit with Mr. Edewor gives hope. I strongly feel that by the time both the Urhobo Union and Sapele Union hear your story, there must be a connection to your family. Don't you feel so?"

"Yes," Mofe and I responded together.

"And I feel so much peace and hope with Mr. Edewor's plan," I added.

"I am confident that his plan to report the matter to the two town unions will ensure success," Mofe said.

"Okay, great. Now that we all agree, Sarah, you need to stop worrying. All will be well," Mrs. Akinyemi concluded.

We sipped our drinks in silence for a few minutes.

Mofe then stood up, looked at me, and I got up too. We thanked and bade Mrs. Akinyemi goodbye.

Our journey back to Mofe's house was something else. The sun was now blazing. You could hardly look up at the sky, as the intensity of the sun was almost blinding. You could feel its fierceness on your skin.

As the day evolved, it seemed as if more vehicles and human traffic had been invited to flood the road. The traffic was so heavy, and both vehicles and people moved so fast that I wondered how we would be able to cross the dual carriageway to get to our bus stop, which Mofe said was on the other side of the four-lane expressway.

When I hesitated at the point we could have used to cross amidst the rushing traffic, Mofe tugged at me and said, "Sorry, Sarah, sweet, we are not going to jump through this mad traffic and that road divider. There is a footbridge just a pole or so away on our right. We are using the footbridge. There is also a bus stop near it."

"Oh, okay. Thanks for being here. I agonized as we approached the road, wondering how we were going to cross amidst this madness called traffic. But see, ooo—some people are jumping across the divide! Look at that woman throwing her legs open, trying to climb through. That's so awful."

"Yes, it is awful. I did not want my Sarah to do that. That's why, as we were approaching the road, I thought it would be best for us to walk to the footbridge, even if it was a kilometer away," Mofe said.

"Hmmmm! Now, Mofe, I am not happy with you."

"O! Sarah, sweet, why na?" Mofe asked.

"Why did you wait until now to come into my life? If you had been there from the beginning, I wouldn't have gone through the hell I have in my short life," I said.

"Let's just say that if you hadn't gone through all these things, I wouldn't have found an angel to be by my side today. Everything works for good for those who love God, as the Bible says," Mofe stated.

"What do you mean?" I queried.

"I mean that you were just journeying to come and meet me— because I love God," Mofe said.

"Does that mean you love God and I don't? And that you're responsible for all my sufferings, right?" I asked.

"Yes," Mofe replied.

"Did you not know that I was traumatized, destroyed? That sometimes I feel worthless given all that I have been through? And that I fear you may judge me and not truly trust or love me?" I asked.

"Sarah, sweet, I believe and practice what the scriptures say: 'Judge not, that ye be not judged.' You have told me your story. Have you noticed anything in my behavior that suggests I do not trust and love you?"

"Nooo! Mofe. I am so happy to have you in my life. Without you, I have no life. I am comforted. Dear Mofe, thank you," I said.

"Not at all, Sarah, sweet. I want you to be at peace with me and around me," Mofe said.

"Oooh, okaaay. Cross my heart, I will remember that, Mofe Makanjuola," I said.

The rest of the journey back to Mofe's house was in silence. We crossed to the other side of the road using the footbridge a few poles away from the Meiron Estate Gate—the same one we used to visit Mrs. Akinyemi.

I continued to feel cozy throughout the day, breaking into song a few times as I busied myself with house chores, including washing Mofe's clothes. Sometimes, Mofe joined in mockingly. Other times, he joined when I sang a Christian chant he was familiar with and liked.

That night, I slept in his arms and would have gladly surrendered my body to him if he had asked. I had learned not to desire sexual intimacy with Mofe, lest I misinterpret his refusal. But I was willing to give in anytime he so much as showed interest.

We slept most of Sunday, as Mofe was not a church-going enthusiast.

Each day throughout the week seemed like an eternity. To show my gratitude, I resisted the urge to complain. And just as day is followed by night, and night by day, Sunday came again, and my tension rose higher. I was on edge all morning. Mofe noticed and begged me to calm down until evening, when we hoped to hear from Mr. Edewor.

At 7 p.m. that evening, Mr. Edewor called Mofe and told him there was good news.

"Tell me about it, sir!" Mofe practically shouted.

"Mofe! Mofe!! Mofe!!! What did he say?" I interrupted.

Mofe hushed me as gently as he could and then put the phone on speaker.

"I have good news for you," Mr. Edewor said from the other end.

I drew closer to Mofe and held him tight, as if that would help me hear more.

"There is information about one Mr. Odafe Enoch Odafe, who circulated a notice about his missing daughter three years ago. Her name is Sarah.

"The said Mr. Enoch was released from prison four years ago under a prerogative of mercy from the Governor of the State. He moved to Sango Ota in Ogun State near Lagos with his wife and son.

"He had sent out a message about his missing daughter, Sarah, which was shared among the Urhobo and Sapele Town Unions four years ago. This must be your Sarah.

"Some people who know him promised to get your message across to him, and I gave them your phone number so he can contact you directly. I hope that is okay with you," Mr. Edewor concluded.

"Oh, that is perfectly okay with me, sir," Mofe responded.

"Is Sarah there with you?" Mr. Edewor asked.

"Yes, she is here with me, sir," Mofe said.

"Oh, okay. Greet her for me. I am happy that your visit to my house is yielding results. I love successful conclusions," Mr. Edewor added.

"Yes, sir! Yes, sir!! Thank you," Mofe and I chorused.

"Yes! Yes!!" I screamed, jumping on Mofe and unabashedly planting a long kiss on his lips. He gasped and returned the kiss. I felt transported to the seventh heaven in that moment.

"So, my days of wandering up and down the streets of this land I now know as Lagos have come to an end—all thanks to this great guy, Mr. Mofe Makanjuola.

"Oh God, I thank you! Please bless Mofe for me, that every good thing he ever desires will come to be in his life—just as he has helped me achieve the greatest dream of my life," I said, with tears of joy running down my cheeks.

Chapter Thirteen

The days following that phone call from Mr. Edewor were like no other in my life. I was in daily—no, hourly—no, in fact, every second was a turmoil of anticipation and upheaval as I awaited the meeting with my parents.

A thousand and one questions flooded my mind. How is my mother now? Did she recover her senses, or is she still in bad shape? How tall is my little brother James now? And my great father—the man who had to endure humiliation because he dared to stand up for his daughter, who had been abused and robbed of her innocence?

The lack of answers to these questions was suffocating the peace and hope I should have felt after hearing the news of a possible reunion with my family.

Every single moment, I anticipated a call from my father, and the wait was excruciating—like hellfire. The anticipation was killing me. Though I managed to prepare the house and meals to warmly welcome Mofe home from work, my soul was restless every second. As usual, Mofe noticed.

"Sarah, sweet, how was your day today?" Mofe asked after I greeted him that evening, lacking my usual energy.

"I don't know," I responded sullenly.

Stretching out his hands toward me, Mofe said, "Sarah, sweet, I can feel that you're worrying yourself sick. There's really no point in that. In my opinion, God has answered our prayers. It's only a matter of days before we hear from your father. Can you please try to stay positive and hopeful?"

Like a charged keg of gunpowder, I exploded—not with words, but with tears.

"Mofe, waiting for that phone call from my father, with a thousand and one questions fighting in my head, is tearing me to shreds," I managed to say through sobs.

"Believe me, Sarah, sweet, I understand. I'm also anxious for that phone call. At work today, every time my phone rang, my heart jumped in anticipation—until I saw the caller's name," Mofe said.

"Ohhh, Mofe, I love you. Thank you for putting yourself in my shoes during this trying time," I said, falling into his warm embrace.

Mofe rocked me gently until I felt at peace enough to give him a grateful peck on the cheek.

The rest of the week was a whirlwind. Every day, my anticipation grew. Each evening, as Mofe returned from work, I would greet him eagerly, hoping for news that my father had called—but to no avail. My hopes and faith in Mr. Edewor's promise of someone reaching out to my father began to wane. As my hope of reuniting with my family through Mr. Edewor's efforts faded, my mood worsened. Tears and tantrums ruled my days, especially when Mofe returned home without any news. But Mofe—oh, my dear Mofe—he has a heart large enough to take it all in. He is a rare gem.

That Friday night was different. A peaceful feeling wrapped around me like a warm blanket, unlike anything I had known in my adult life. I slept like a baby. When I woke up, I found myself singing Christian chants, which startled Mofe awake. He came over from the sitting room, where he had been sleeping, to check on me.

"Sarah, sweet, you're singing?" he asked, surprised.

"Yes, Mofe, dear. Since last night, I've felt this deep, cozy peace that has me singing this morning," I responded.

"Ahh! Glory be to God!" Mofe exclaimed, his excitement clear.

That morning, I busied myself with house chores—washing Mofe's clothes, cleaning up the house, cooking—all while singing. Mofe and I prepared breakfast together, and from time to time, he stole glances at me as if he were dreaming. Eventually, he voiced his thoughts.

"Sarah, sweet, is this really you?" he asked.

"Yes, Mofe dear, it's me. Why do you ask?" I said, amused.

"Did you win the lottery or something?" he teased.

"I don't know ooo," I said, laughing.

"Well, Sarah, sweet, whatever it is, I want you to stay like this every second, every minute, every day, and forever with me," Mofe said.

"Amen, amen, amen!" I responded.

"I'll take you out this afternoon to celebrate this wonderful feeling and atmosphere in the house. Do you like the idea?" Mofe asked.

The sun rose early that Saturday morning. Before 7:00 a.m., it had already spread its golden light across the earth, warming everything in sight.

I recalled a saying from the Igbo people I had lived among when I was younger: "Ubochi oma jiri ututu wara anwu," which means, "A good day starts with an early sunrise." I decided to share this with Mofe.

"Mofe, my Igbo neighbors always say that when the sun rises early in the morning, it's a sign of a good day," I said.

"I agree ooo! You woke up singing before 6:00 a.m., and the sun is already bright and warm. I hope this brings us luck, just like your neighbors used to say," Mofe replied.

"Amen! Amen!! Amen!!!" I echoed.

We had breakfast with a joy I hadn't felt in days. I held Mofe's hand throughout most of the meal. Once we finished, we carried the dishes to the kitchen and washed them together.

Afterward, I took a bath. Mofe had promised to take me out for lunch to celebrate the peace and happiness we had been feeling all day.

The sun blazed relentlessly. Because the restaurant was a bit far, and we would have had to walk under the intense heat, we decided to push our outing to the evening.

By 5:45 p.m., though the heat had softened, the sunset still blazed on the horizon. We had just taken our seats at the restaurant when Mofe's phone rang. It was an unregistered number.

Mofe answered.

"Yes, sir, this is Mofe Makanjuola. Who is speaking, and how may I help you?"

A deep voice responded, "This is Mr. Odafe Enoch Odafe…"

"Hold on, sir, let me put the phone on speaker. We have been expecting your call all week," Mofe interrupted.

"I am Sarah's father," my father said. "My townsman just gave me your number now and reported that you are with my daughter, Sarah. Is that true? Is she there with you?"

I screamed. "Yes, Papa! Yes, Papa!! I am here. How are you, Papa? How is my mother? How is James? Where are you all?" I kept asking amid sobs, without waiting for any answers.

"Sarah, my jewel, I give glory to God today for making it possible to hear your voice again in this life. I have feared and suffered much, thinking I would never see you again. Your mother and your brother, James, are all here with me, and we are all doing well and happy to hear from you again. How are you doing?" my father said and asked at the same time.

Before I could answer my father's question, I heard that unmistakable voice of my mother singing:

"He has done for me, he has done for me, he has done for me, he has done for me.

What my mother cannot do, he has done for me.

What my father cannot do, he has done for meee oooo."

"Sarah ooooo! Sarah oooooo!!" my mother screamed.

My brother, James, joined in, screaming and crying, "Sister, Sister!" Their voices made it obvious they were crying.

Can you imagine a riot of emotions? That's the only way I can describe my condition. I was happy. I was sorrowful. At the same time, I was worried sick about my mother's condition.

"Ooohhh! Mama!! I have missed you. I am happy to hear your voice again in this life. I have been overtaken by fear that I may never see you all again. Oh, God!! Oh, Mofe!! My heart is filled with thanks for this day, which I have cried, prayed, hoped, and sorrowed for—it has finally come."

"Papa! Where are you? I want to see you all now, today. Is your place near or far?" I asked.

"We live at Sango Ota. Our house is close to the highway. Where are you so I can know how close you are to us?" my father asked.

Before I could turn to Mofe—faithful Mofe—he took over the conversation.

"Sir, we live at Iyana Ipaja. What is the nearest landmark to your house? I think we can come to Sango Ota today despite the traffic on that road," said Mofe.

"We live right by the Catholic Church, almost at the foot of the Sango Ota Interchange when you cross it. Our place is on the right of you as you come from Iyana Ipaja. Today is Saturday. The traffic jam will be there, but it won't be too bad. If you start now, I believe you will make it in good time. We can't wait to see Sarah again," my father stated.

"We will be on our way now, then. Thank you, sir!" Mofe said.

"Very well, Mr. Makanjuola. God bless you for us," my father said as he ended the call.

"Sarah Sweet, you have a choice now. You either sit down and have the meal I promised you or travel to Sango Ota to see your parents and James. What will it be?" Mofe quipped.

"Whaaat! That is mean of you, Mofe," I said, feigning serious anger at his statement, though I understood it as a joke.

"It was only a joke, please," Mofe said.

"Okay, Mr. 'Jokey' Makanjuola, keep the food and take me to my family jọọ," I said, smiling with tears still flowing.

"Okay, Sarah 'Serious,' we must pass through the house and get some overnight clothing. I suspect some people will not be able to sleep in Iyana Ipaja tonight," Mofe said.

"Me? 'Sarah Serious?' Okay. Just wait until I set my eyes on my parents and little brother James—I will redefine our relationship and make you pay," I said, smiling and truly happy.

We packed a backpack from the house, containing one T-shirt, a pair of jeans, and underwear for Mofe, along with two days' worth of clothes for me.

Trust Mofe to make smart decisions. Instead of going to the bus stop to catch a bus, he called a taxi, which charged us N3,500 for a direct trip. When I questioned the expense, Mofe explained that buses would take ages due to traffic, frequent stops, and picking up passengers.

As we covered a few kilometers, Mofe suddenly screamed, "Hey! Sarah Sweet, we didn't buy any bread for James and your mom."

"Oh! Really? Should we?" I asked.

"I think it's wise," Mofe said.

He asked the driver to take us to a nearby supermarket so we could get some things for James and my parents. We entered a supermarket about half a kilometer from where we made the decision and bought provisions, including two big loaves of bread, groundnuts, cashew nuts, milk, chocolate, avocados, carrots, biscuits, and more.

When we arrived at the Catholic Church premises, Mofe called my father's phone to inform him that we were there. My father told us to wait, and he would come to get us.

Mofe paid the taxi driver, who then left, and we stood there for a minute or two. Then my father—my hero and my cheerleader—emerged from the metal gate right beside the Catholic Church. Upon seeing me, he started running and calling out:

"Sarah!

Sarah!!

My mother!!!

My jewel!!!!"

I turned and saw him—my father, the lanky, athletic man now adorned with gray hairs. I ran toward him, tears flowing nonstop. I rushed into his outstretched arms, and he grabbed me. We clung to each other, using each other to stabilize ourselves.

"Oh, God of Heaven, thank you for making this day possible! That I, Odafe Enoch Odafe, with my eyes and my hands, can behold and touch this angel you blessed me with eighteen years ago—whom I lost for more than seven years now," my father exclaimed.

"Oh, my father. My hero. My cheerleader. I have missed you," I cried. "Where is my mother and my little brother, James? How are they doing? Are they in the house?"

"Yes, dear. They are in the house. They are waiting for you. I told them to wait so I could bring you home myself," my father said.

For a moment, I forgot that Mofe was still there. Then my father said, "This must be Mr. Mofe Makanjuola."

"Yes! Yes!! Yes!!! Papa," I said.

"Come here, my son," my father said, beckoning Mofe over.

My father released me and shook hands with Mofe before pulling him close and hugging him tightly, tapping his back.

"Thank you. Thank you. Thank you, my son. You have done what Napoleon could not do. Thank you. Thank you. Thank you."

"Now, let's go home. My wife and James are waiting," my father said.

Mofe picked up the backpack and the bag containing our purchases from the supermarket.

Meeting my mother after all these years, knowing she had nearly lost her mind during the incident, put me in a state of emotional agitation. But for over seven years, I had yearned for this moment—to be with my mother again. Here was my chance. I just needed to brace myself, face it, and meet this great woman who gave me life and protected me the best she could.

My mother and James were waiting outside the door inside the compound. As soon as I entered, both of them screamed and raced toward me, and I ran toward them. The three of us were enveloped in an embrace—so warm, so teary, and so rapturous.

"Sarah Enoch, the jewel of her father! Is this you? Oh, God of heaven, did you permit me to see my angel again in this life? All glory and honor be unto You, my unfailing God!" my mother cried out with joy.

"Sister! Sister! I have missed you," James cried.

My father joined us and then led us inside.

It was a three-bedroom, semi-detached bungalow in a nice location. The compound had interlocking tiles, and my parents' apartment had flowerpots in front of it. The sitting room was sparkling clean. Though modest, the furniture and fittings were tasteful. Four potted flowers stood in each corner of the room. This was a much more prosperous living situation than we had known before. My parents must have done well for themselves, recovering from the trauma of everything that happened after the day I was viciously raped.

Surprisingly, my mother still looked beautiful, though her face showed some signs of aging. She still carried herself with the same confidence I had always known.

My preteen brother, James, seemed too tall for his age. It was obvious he was taking after our father.

Once we settled down, my mother turned to Mofe and asked, "You must be Mofe Makanjuola—the one who saved our angel and brought her back to us?"

"Yes, Mama. Sarah has told me so much about you. I'm glad to finally meet you," Mofe responded.

"My God will bless you. Whatever you seek from Him, He will grant you. May the sun shine before you every day! May your shadow never grow less!" My mother continued to pour blessings upon Mofe.

"Amin! Amin! Amin!" Mofe replied.

"Sarah, join me in the kitchen so we can make food and talk more," my mother commanded, fully in her element.

That statement sent shivers down my spine and made me happy at the same time. It reminded me of my early years with her. She had a commanding voice and presence that could never be mistaken. Seeing her in this state made me happy—I felt she was fully healed and back to her true self.

I jumped at the chance to be alone with my mother, eager to feel her warmth again and find out how she had managed all these years. However, I dreaded the inevitable questions about where I had been and how I had survived. That would be a difficult conversation. If I still knew my mother, she wouldn't wait until tomorrow to ask. For her, everything happened in the moment, which made me nervous about being alone with her.

I reached her side, attached myself to her arm, and we walked into the kitchen like Siamese twins.

"Sarah," my mother called. "I know you're expecting me to ask you how you managed all these years. But that's a long story, and I don't want to distract from the joy of seeing you again. However…" She paused, giving me a knowing look. "I couldn't help noticing how you and that young man, Mofe, look at each other. So, what's up? Are you two in love?"

"Ahh! Ma…ma! I can't remember doing or saying anything to warrant such a question!" I countered.

"Sarah Enoch, do you think I'm a baby? I was just 18 when I married your father. I have an eye for these things, dear," she said.

"Well, Mama, apart from the fact that Mofe saved my life, I have grown to love him. He hasn't told me he loves me, but the way he treats me…I believe he wants me in his life. He goes to great lengths for me," I admitted.

"Are you both having sex? Are you pregnant?" my mother shot at me.

I was flabbergasted, and it showed. My mother widened her eyes and pressed on.

"Ehn ehn! Answer me, joo, Sarah!"

"Not yet, Mama. He is too much of a gentleman. I've even offered myself to him to show gratitude for his care and love, but he has refused every time. He says his mother taught him to respect women and never to take advantage of one under any circumstance.

He and his sister were raised single-handedly by his widowed mother from a tender age."

"Wow! Wow!!" My mother clapped her hands together. "His type is rare. Hold him well, ooo!"

"Is this my mother or someone else speaking? Wait, let me check and be sure I returned to the right home," I joked, turning my mother around and looking directly into her face.

"Sarah, I know what you mean. I'm sorry. The circumstances of the past several years have changed me. And after all, you're now a grown woman." Tears streamed down her face.

My mother normally wouldn't have broached the topic of relationships, let alone sex. I suppose I learned from her example.

"It's okay, Mama," I said, hugging her. "We have all changed. We are all changing. In these past few years, I have learned enough to understand the true meaning of your efforts in raising me. And you know what, Mrs. Enoch? I love you."

"Oh, my God! My daughter has become an understanding woman. It shall be well with you, Sarah," my mother said.

After the wonderful meal my mother painstakingly prepared, my father requested that Mofe tell them about himself.

Mofe then added, "I need to begin my journey back home to avoid traveling at night. I don't like staying out late."

"Oh, Mofe! Do you mean you're going to abandon me here among these total strangers? Where are you going when I need you the most?" I joked.

"Sarah Sweet, I am not abandoning you. Since tomorrow is Sunday, I'll return in the morning and stay until evening. You need time with your family. Is there anything I should bring for you from the house tomorrow?"

"You seem so happy to run away and leave me here, right, Mofe?"

"Why do you think I'm returning early tomorrow morning? Don't finish the breakfast your mom is going to prepare for you. Do you hear?"

"Oh! Now that makes sense. Dream about me, ooo!" I teased.

"Sarah Sweet, it's going to be more than a dream. My real soul will remain here with you. I'm just taking my body," Mofe said.

"Awww! That feels cool, Mofe," I replied.

My father walked us to the door, and I walked Mofe to the Catholic Church, where he told me to return home before I got lost in the crazy Sango Ota Flyover Bridge traffic.

"I don't want to be held responsible for someone's daughter going missing a second time," he said.

"Come on, Mofe Makanjuola, be nice to me a little, na. Abegi," I said playfully.

He grabbed me and gave me a hug—the kind that said, *I'm missing you already.* Then he raced off, smartly navigating the fast-moving Sango Ota traffic while exiting the overhead bridge. I watched until he safely crossed to the bus stop. As soon as he turned back to look at me, I blew him a kiss and returned home.

As I returned to the house, my mother was waiting for me in the sitting room. Smiling and obviously excited, she greeted me and bid me to sit down.

"You are in love with him, Sarah?" she asked with obvious interest.

"Yes, Mama, I love Mofe. Do I really have a choice when a man has devoted the past few months to doing nothing else but wiping away my tears, loving me, caring for me, and giving me back my family?" I said, asking at the same time.

My mother stretched out her hands, and I fell into them. Our hearts beat together, and I felt that unspoken understanding only mothers and daughters share. She rocked me, and that made me feel even more confident in my decision to invest my emotions in my relationship with Mofe.

When we disentangled, I discovered that tears of joy had been running down our faces.

We spent a lot of time reminiscing about our past without each other. We cried. We hugged. We laughed. We rejoiced. We reconnected our souls and became a family again.

We hardly had time for dinner, but my mother quickly put together some snacks—groundnuts, cucumber, banana, and apple—which became our dinner as we munched and chatted away late into the night.

At 3:00 a.m., James finally fell asleep, and the rest of us were obviously tired. My father called for a truce, suggesting we continue our conversation the next day after sacrament meeting.

"What is sacrament meeting?" I asked.

"It is our church meeting," my father responded.

"Oh! Ok!!" I said.

Chapter Fourteen

MOFE was already knocking at our door by 7:30 a.m. My father had woken all of us up at 6:00 a.m., despite just going to bed at 3:00 a.m. He said we needed to prepare for Sacrament Meeting that morning.

I was excited that Mofe was already here so early. I imagined he probably hadn't slept that night, thinking and worrying about losing me now that I had my family. I felt good—desirable, even.

I got the door, and there stood Mofe with that look that tells you you've been sorely missed. I decided to play games with him.

"Mofe, did you even sleep last night?" I asked.

"Sleep? How is that even possible without you?" he replied.

"Why is that? You're not even married to me, and you're having sleepless nights over a woman you haven't married," I teased.

"You're asking me why? So, are you telling me that you were happy to let me go? That when I left, you had all the peace and quiet you wanted and enjoyed your sleep?" Mofe asked, his voice changing.

"Not so fast, Mr. Mofe Makanjuola," I said in my usual alluring way, emphasizing how happy I was with him. "I didn't sleep a wink either. Can't you see my tired face? First, we talked all night until 3:00 a.m., and then my father woke us all up at 6:00 a.m. to prepare for church. Do you know what I did from 3:00 to 6:00 a.m.?"

"Nooo! Give me a piece of the meat," he said.

"Once I was alone this morning, all I thought about was you. At first, I only wondered whether you got home safely. Then I wondered if you were sleeping or not. Then I wished I was with you. Oh, how painful it was to realize that you were elsewhere. I missed you so much, Mofe," I said.

"I missed you too, Sarah Sweet," Mofe said as we embraced.

I took some of my clothes and other things he had brought for me, including biscuits, bread, apples, carrots, cucumbers, and groundnuts. I gave him another hug for remembering to bring me the snacks I love.

I asked him to sit and wait for us to be ready for church, then announced to my dad and mom that Mofe was here. They expressed pleasant surprise.

By 8:00 a.m., Mother was ready with breakfast. My father had announced that breakfast was at 8:00 a.m. sharp and that we would leave the house at 8:30 a.m. Our church was just a 15-minute walk away and started at 9:00 a.m.

I spent some time watching my brother, James, as he rushed through his breakfast. When I asked him why, he explained that the rule in our house on Sunday mornings was that breakfast must be finished by 8:30 a.m. because that was when we had to leave for Sacrament Meeting.

Mofe and I exchanged a glance and quickly finished our breakfast.

When my father joined us, he invited Mofe to come to church with us if he wished. Otherwise, he was welcome to wait at home. Mofe volunteered to come, which made me very happy.

The experience at church was exquisite. It was a small congregation of fewer than 200 people meeting in a rented twin block of flats. The members were warm and welcoming, greeting everyone with smiles.

The bishop and those seated with him on the pulpit were dressed simply—white shirts and ties, with two of them wearing suits.

Mofe and I sat close to my father. At the end of the meeting, many people came over to greet my parents and asked about the visitors with them—meaning Mofe and me.

My father proudly introduced me as his daughter, Sarah, and introduced Mofe as my friend, Mr. Mofe Makanjuola.

Some people recognized my story and asked if I was the missing child. My father confirmed that I was. They immediately began thanking God for preserving my life.

I hadn't spent much of my life in church, but being among these people was such a sweet experience.

I watched Mofe to see if I could read his feelings about the experience. He seemed to be paying close attention to everything.

At the end of the meetings, as people lingered to greet one another, I asked Mofe what he thought. He said he had never had an experience like this in a church before. He noted that everything was different from what he had known about churches and said he would be glad to learn more.

Just then, two young women with name tags reading "The Church of Jesus Christ of Latter-day Saints" approached us.

They introduced themselves as missionaries and asked if we were new to the church and whether we would like to learn more about it.

Mofe and I turned to look at each other at the same time—we both felt we should. So, we told the missionaries we would like to learn more.

They gave us a brief introduction to their beliefs and teachings. Then, they took our names and Mofe's phone number so they could contact us and plan further discussions. They also invited us to return next Sunday and offered to teach us at Brother Odafe's home or at the chapel, whichever we preferred.

When we returned home that afternoon, I asked my father how he had come to join this church.

He explained that while he was in prison, members of the church had come for prison fellowship. After worshiping together, they asked if anyone felt they had been wrongly imprisoned.

After struggling with his conscience, he felt compelled to share his story. Though he was guilty of the charge against him, he believed he should have been pardoned out of mercy, given the circumstances of his case.

After hearing his story, the church members spoke with the prison officials. The officials confirmed that my father's behavior was not that of a murderer—he had been exemplary in his work and in maintaining peace in the prison.

A few weeks later, the church members returned and told him they had reviewed his case with lawyers. They all agreed to apply for a prerogative of mercy from the governor of Ekiti State.

They prepared his case, emphasizing that his wife had lost her mind and his two children were missing because of his imprisonment.

The governor granted the request, and my father was pardoned under the prerogative of mercy, which resides with the governor of the state.

That's how he regained his freedom. By the grace of God, he found my mother, and as soon as she saw him, she got well. She had never been unwell since that day.

They looked for James at my aunt's place and found him. They also discovered that my aunt had died months earlier from a heart attack—and that I was missing.

They took James, relocated here, and had been trying to rebuild their lives, praying every day that they would see me again.

The leaders of the church stayed close to them, supporting them in every way. The missionaries taught them the gospel, and they accepted it.

Their life had been wonderful ever since—only punctuated by my absence.

They had been planning to go to the temple to seal their marriage and their family, as required by God. But my father said something kept telling him to wait—that they would find me, and if I joined the church, we could do it together.

"Beholding you with my own eyes and touching you with my own hands again, my jewel, is a sign that God lives and answers prayers," he said. "I wish and pray that you will listen to the missionaries. If you find their teachings right for you and join the church, we can go to the temple in Aba, Abia State, Nigeria, to be sealed together for time and all eternity."

I felt happy hearing my father's story and how everything had unfolded.

To my surprise, Mofe said he wanted to investigate the church with me. And if I decided to join, he would join too.

Chapter Fifteen

Every Saturday, Mofe would come to our house in the morning. We would spend the whole day together, and the missionaries would teach us the gospel.

Some Saturdays, I would go home with him so we could be together and so I could take care of his house, plan his meals for the week or the next few weeks. I would cook for him for the coming week and then return home in the evening. Sometimes, if it was late, he would bring me home and then return to his own house.

Every Sunday morning, Mofe would arrive at our house at 7:30 a.m. We would have breakfast together and go to church. After church, we would spend the whole Sunday at our home, and in the evening, Mofe would return to his own house.

My parents were excited about Mofe and the possibility of him becoming their son-in-law. From time to time, my mother would ask me if I was keeping myself virtuous. According to her, we should not break the law of chastity as members of the Church. Plus, she would say, *"I do not want you to marry because of pregnancy. You need to marry because you love your man, and he loves you—and he, by himself, asks you to marry him. The only reason I got pregnant before wedding your father was because my parents refused to allow him to marry me. Otherwise, both of us loved each other, and he had proposed to me, and I accepted. It was our parents who refused. I had to find a way, so I asked him to make me pregnant so that my parents would have no choice but to agree."*

I always reassured her. I let her know that if it were up to me, I would have been having sex with Mofe. But Mofe would not have any of that. He is the greatest man on earth. I still wonder if he is real because everyone who had offered to help me during my journey in the wilderness had their way with me on the first day of our meeting.

We met with the missionaries for another five weeks, and both Mofe and I decided that we should get baptized.

The very Saturday of our baptism was a day I looked forward to with reasonable excitement. One of my reasons was that Mofe had decided we should join the Church. However, the best part of what happened was something I totally did not expect. Perhaps my parents, along with Mofe's mother and sister, knew ahead of time.

First, I had been feeling good about membership in the Church, given the simplicity of their approach, the teachings, the cordiality of the members, and my parents' devoted excitement about it.

Second, I was thrillingly shocked to see Mofe's mother and sister arrive with him at our home that morning for the baptism. I had not known that he was telling them about the Church and everything that was happening. I was truly surprised to see them. But that was still a small matter.

In my usual spirit, the day started with me waking up early and feeling noticeably happy. I could not put my finger on why I was so happy, but I just was.

The sun rose early that morning, as is usual in Lagos during the dry season. By 6:00 a.m., sunlight had already pierced through the window blinds, casting a kaleidoscope of colors across my bed and onto the opposite wall. The sight was multi-colored and heartwarming to behold. But nothing warned me about what was coming.

Mofe, my father—who was acting as John the Baptist for the day—and I were dressed in knee-length white tunics and white trousers for the baptism.

The baptismal service was simple but deeply exciting for me. My father baptized me first and then Mofe. We emerged from the dressing room beaming with smiles and joy.

After announcing the remaining formalities, the bishop, who was present at the baptismal service, added that a special event would take place before we started the next segment of the service.

He then announced, *"Mr. Mofe Makanjuola has a special announcement to make."*

Though I wondered what "special" announcement Mofe was about to make, I was not particularly concerned since I had never attended a baptismal service before. Instead, I was simply apprehensive for him, hoping he would be able to do whatever was required of him. So, I watched him intently as he stood up.

You can imagine my shock when he turned, knelt before me, and proposed.

"Sarah, Sweet, will you marry me?" he asked.

I looked at my father beside me, and he nodded cheerfully. I turned toward my mother and my little brother, James, who were sitting nearby. My mother nodded her approval with a smile, while James grinned. Then I turned to Mofe's mother and sister, who were seated behind us. Both of them nodded in agreement, as if they had known ahead of time what was going to happen.

With tears of joy streaming down my cheeks, I said,

"Yes. Yes. Mofe, I will marry you today, tomorrow, and forevermore."

For the rest of the meeting, I leaned on Mofe's shoulder, and my whole world felt complete again—just as it had before I was raped by Tunde.

Everyone clapped. And there was joy!

References

1. Azuonwu, Oliver O. Bishop. Quote at a talk delivered at a Church meeting of the Umuchichi Ward of the Aba Nigeria Stake of The Church of Jesus Christ of Latter-day Saints, Aba, 2012.

2. Popular saying.

3. Job 3:25, King James Version (KJV), The Holy Bible, The Church of Jesus Christ of Latter-day Saints.

4. Popular expression. Matthew 7:1-3, King James Version (KJV), The Holy Bible, The Church of Jesus Christ of Latter-day Saints.

9 781967 441457